Dear Readers,

Mother Nature may have turned up the heat, but nothing could be hotter than four sizzling new romances from Bouquet.

Get ready for two very different weddings! *Affaire de Coeur* raved about Suzanne Barrett's first Bouquet. This month she offers **Wild Irish Rogue,** a lively romp involving a green card, a favor of the matrimonial kind—and, of course, true love. In **The Bride's Best Man,** veteran Meteor author Laura Phillips gives us the story of a woman preparing to walk down the aisle—and wondering if her sexy childhood friend is really the man who should be at her side.

No one can pick out a bridal gown until she finds the right man—even if she finds him in the most unexpected place. A single dad is **Falling for Grace** in Maddie James's latest offering about neighbors who can get close in the sweetest way possible. Finally, a legacy of love and a decades-old jewel heist provide the backdrop for one clashing couple's **Stolen Kisses** from Kate Donovan.

Why not pack a Bouquet in your beach bag and let us show you just how good romance can be?

Kate Duffy
Editorial Director

## "WE'VE NEVER DONE THIS BEFORE, HAVE WE?"

Jack's voice, close to her ear, sent a delicious shiver down Marcy's spine. Not chill, but intensely warm and exciting. The sensation unnerved her.

"Why not?" he added.

She swallowed back the lump forming in her throat. "Maybe because you always chose your partners for their bra size instead of their skill at tying a knot in fishing line."

A soft sigh whispered from Jack's lips. "There are some things a guy just doesn't do with his best friend. Women come and go, but a friend is different."

*Friend.* He'd said friend, and that's what he was—her best friend. Reminding herself of that didn't ease the rapid beating of her heart, or the comfortable rightness in the feel of his hands about her waist. It didn't make her stop wanting to lean closer against him.

Her fingers shifted restlessly, and she noticed his pulse beating beneath her thumb, in time with her own racing heart. Then she began to tremble. This was not how a woman was supposed to feel in the arms of her best friend.

# THE BRIDE'S BEST MAN

## Laura Phillips

Zebra Books
Kensington Publishing Corp.
http://www.zebrabooks.com

ZEBRA BOOKS are published by

Kensington Publishing Corp.
850 Third Avenue
New York, NY 10022

Copyright © 2000 by Laura Phillips

All rights reserved. No part of this book may be reproduced in any form or by any means without the prior written consent of the Publisher, excepting brief quotes used in reviews.

If you purchased this book without a cover you should be aware that this book is stolen property. It was reported as "unsold and destroyed" to the Publisher and neither the Author nor the Publisher has received any payment for this "stripped book."

Zebra and the Z logo Reg. U.S. Pat. & TM Off.

First Printing: July, 2000
10 9 8 7 6 5 4 3 2 1

Printed in the United States of America

# ONE

Never had a day been so perfect.

A light breeze skimmed across the water, barely rippling the surface. Songbirds twittered among the background buzz of bees nuzzling wildflowers for pollen.

Fifty feet offshore, a huge bass leaped into the air and landed with a splash tantamount to a challenge.

Jack Rathert stood at the edge of the water and grinned. He never had been one to ignore a challenge.

A quick glance at his watch told him it was well past his fishing buddy's usual arrival time. Apparently, he'd be fishing alone today. Again.

Too bad. Jack missed their Saturday morning sessions, a little bragging, a little fishing, maybe a cool drink afterward to celebrate the big catch—or the lack of any catch. Plus, it would have been nice to have somebody around to take the classic trophy picture when he landed that big boy out there.

Jack adjusted his favorite fishing hat and reached into the back of his truck for his favorite fishing rod and new open reel. In less than ten minutes, he was perched on a rock outcrop at the lake's edge, casting in the direction of the big fish's last leap.

An hour later, he'd hooked two keepers and thrown back three others. The big fellow or one of his equally large buddies had jumped twice more, teasing Jack with the promise of what awaited just beyond the ripples from his last cast. Jack was switching lures when the fish splashed again, much closer to shore.

Behind him the underbrush rustled. A hint of jasmine mingled with the woodsy scents that had been there all along. He didn't need to turn around to determine the intruder's identity.

"Marcy Winters, you're late again," he said, more pleased than irritated. He'd missed her, missed their talks. Nobody could straighten out his mind like Marcy.

Her low, throaty chuckle made his throat tighten. The sensation caught him by surprise, although it shouldn't have. It hit him now and then, stole his voice for a fraction of a second before he could put the feelings back in that little locked cabinet in the corner of his mind.

"You'd think I would have outgrown the urge to sneak up behind you and push you into the lake," she said. "Maybe if I managed to dunk you, the urge would go away."

"You make too much noise," he told her, keeping the real secret to himself. Some things you didn't tell even your best friend. No sense in giving away his advantage.

"Yeah, yeah, I know. I guess I'll never be one with the wind." Marcy adjusted her battered cap as she moved past him and gazed out across the water. "Boy, what I wouldn't give to get that baby on the end of my line."

"Really? You could have fooled me." An hour and a half late and she hadn't even brought a pole. He finished with the lure and swung his arm in an arc, casting wide in his irritation.

"Sorry. I tried to call, but you'd already left. I had good intentions when I got out of bed, but then Roger called. His car broke down, so I had to give him a ride to work."

Roger. The boyfriend with the fine lineage, big expense account, and even bigger ambitions. Too bad he hadn't a practical bone in his body. Otherwise the man wouldn't have bought that flashy car with all those gadgets and features that seemed to keep breaking. The thought triggered a smirk Jack tried hard to control.

"And you can't stay," he surmised. She wore the usual jeans, hiking boots, and shirt, but her lack of fishing gear made her intentions apparent. Nope, Marcy Winters had bigger fish to fry than the ones leaping in these waters today.

She bit her lip and turned away. "Not today," she confirmed. "I wanted to talk to you, though, and this seemed like a good time, a good place." She stepped forward and lifted his stringer, surveying his catch. "It's important, and I wanted you to be the first to know. You are my best friend, after all."

"Since third grade," he agreed, touching the tarnished Girl Scout pin on the crown of his hat—a good luck gift from Marcy when Jack's tonsils had been removed. He watched her for a moment, tallying the little signs of nervousness. Thumb tapping against the tree. The way she avoided his eyes.

"This sounds serious," he said to break the silence that had fallen between them.

"Couldn't be more serious." Still, she didn't elaborate.

"You're taking the job in Minneapolis," he prompted.

"Bigger than that."

"The New York office?"

She laughed. "Yeah, right. The fishing stinks, and they don't allow camping in Central Park. No, it's nothing like that." Her gaze slid away from his. Whatever she had to tell him, she didn't expect him to like it.

An uneasy sensation settled in the pit of his stomach. "You're moving in with Roger."

"No! At least not yet. Eventually, but not until after we're married." She shuffled her feet, then slowly turned to face him.

"Married?" He stood there a moment, clenching the fishing pole as he absorbed the idea. "You're not joking, are you?"

"No, Jack. Roger and I are getting married two months from today."

"Aw, come on. You don't want to do that. You'd be crazy to do something like that," he said before he could help himself. "You know what marriage does to otherwise sane, sensible people."

The words hung between them like a hot blast of summer heat, uncomfortable and inescapable. Disappointment flared in her expression. "Look, Jack, not everyone is as disillusioned and cynical as you."

"Cynical, realistic—what's the difference?" he groused.

"You know there's a difference. You just won't admit that . . . that . . . Jack, you have a bite."

He stared at her. "OK, so I'm a little short-tempered on the subject. But that doesn't mean I'm not right."

"A big one, Jack, a big one!" she exclaimed, rushing closer and grabbing at the pole he'd forgotten he was holding.

He instinctively gripped it tighter. A sudden jerk from the line penetrated his senses, and he turned toward the water. Holy cow, Marcy was right. The reel buzzed, running backward as the fish fought the hook, heading across the cove.

"You're going to lose him," Marcy warned. "He's heading for the brush."

"Hush up and get the net."

"And take the blame if he isn't hooked hard and gets away? Not again. Give me the pole."

"Not in this lifetime, sweetheart."

"Sweetheart my foot," she snapped back, flicking a spray of lake water in his direction.

He ignored her except for a wide grin. Damn, this was more like it. A fine fish on the line and his best friend bantering and standing by with the net. If the last five minutes hadn't happened, he'd have called it a perfect day.

"Small-mouthed or striped?" he called out. They always did that, picked the species like they were calling heads or tails for a coin toss. Whoever won bought coffee afterward.

"Striped, but I can't go," Marcy answered.

"Then I'll take a rain check." Even though she agreed, a feeling too much like regret for Jack's comfort flowed through him. Damn, damn again. He'd wanted to hold on to the camaraderie a little longer. Too soon, she'd have no time at all for him and their simple pleasures. Too soon the sweet days of their friendship would be behind them. Was it too much to ask for just a few more minutes? Maybe not.

With an effort, he pushed his disappointment aside. He needed to land this fish, and right now Marcy was here, watching, waiting, brimming with eagerness just like old times. There'd be time enough for regrets later. Plenty of time.

"Watch it!" Marcy called as she noted the fish's attempt at an end run around a half-submerged log near the shoreline. Jack whipped the rod around, cranking hard to bring him in fast. Then, too soon, it was over. The fish was neatly netted, and Marcy was groaning over her loss.

"You should have known better," Jack said. "Didn't you read the conservation department's fishing report? Striped bass, average length seven inches. This one's twice that."

"I've been busy," she answered slowly, and once again her expression changed to that odd mixture of excitement and caution.

"Yeah, I've noticed." A sigh of exasperation escaped him. This really was an impossible situation. He studied the fish, concentrated on unhooking it while he mouthed the words he didn't want to say. "I suppose congratulations are in order. I hope you'll be very happy."

He meant the last part, at least. He did want her

to be happy. He cared too much not to want the very best for her. The trouble was he didn't think Roger fit that description. Right now probably wouldn't be the time to convince her of that, though, so he kept silent.

The flicker of relief in her expression made him glad he'd made the effort. She smiled, and, for an instant, the sunshine returned to his day.

"I know we'll be happy." A shadow tinged her smile, and Jack's focus sharpened as she drew a deep breath before continuing. "The wedding itself is another story. It's going to be huge. You know how big my family's gatherings are, and then there's Roger's family and all their connections. I need to ask a big favor of you."

Jack couldn't breathe. This was it. Not only was she not going to be his just-a-phone-call-away best buddy anymore, she was going to ask if he minded being left off the invitation list to make room for somebody more important to Roger's future. He stiffened, waiting for the blow. "Ask away," he said, trying not to let his resentment creep into his voice.

"I want you to be my maid of honor."

"Huh?" He couldn't have heard her right.

"Well, I guess 'best man' would be a better term, although that means we'd have two best men, and, well, you know what I mean." She hesitated. "You do know what I mean, don't you?"

He shook his head. She wasn't making any sense at all, at least not to him.

"It's traditional for a girl to ask her best friend to be part of the wedding, to be maid of honor. You're my best friend," she said, as if that explained everything. "Jack, the fish!" she added with a shriek.

He heard her. He registered the sensation of his grip loosening, the sound of the fish falling from his grasp, the splashing flurry as it landed in the very edge of the water.

It flopped around until it landed in water deep enough to right itself, then zipped out of sight into the murky depths of the lake.

"Aw, Jack," Marcy groaned.

Shrugging, he turned his back on the lake. It didn't matter. That fish wasn't the most important thing he'd lost that day.

Maybe all wasn't completely lost, though. She'd asked him to be part of her wedding, and that was no small thing. It wouldn't be easy watching her marry Roger, considering his misgivings about the rightness of the marriage. He would do it, though, and he'd smile and pretend he liked it.

"Marcy," he began, "I'm OK with the honor part and with whatever else you need me to do, keep track of the ring or whatever. Just don't expect me to wear a dress."

She grinned, and Jack thought he detected a shimmer of unshed tears in her eyes. Or maybe it was just excitement, because in the next instant, she launched herself into his arms. "Oh, thank you, Jack. I was so afraid you'd say no and then I'd be stuck with Roger's wasp-tongued sister."

"A fate worse than death," Jack agreed as he tried to ignore the lump in his throat.

She stayed a few minutes more, talking of church dates and fittings. Then she was gone, and Jack was

# THE BRIDE'S BEST MAN

left with his own thoughts. They were poor company. Besides, the luster had gone from the day. So he packed up his gear and headed for town to get an earlier start than he'd planned on the pile of work still waiting on his desk.

Marcy whipped the car into a parking spot outside the restaurant and grimaced at the time on the dashboard clock. She was late for the second time today, and she suspected Roger might be less forgiving than Jack.

"I'm sorry," she muttered as Roger greeted her from where he'd been waiting just inside the foyer of the Ristorante Paris.

"My mother and yours have already been seated. What kept you?" As he spoke, he pressed a hand to the small of her back, steering her into the dining room.

"I drove out to the lake to talk to Jack," she said. Then, before she could lose her courage, she told her fiancé why. His response was less than she'd hoped for.

"I can't believe you asked him without even discussing the matter with me first."

Marcy glanced back at her fiancé's face, noting the faint twitch in his jaw, the only visible sign of his anger. "Did you discuss your choice of best man with me?"

"That's quite different, and you know it."

"Is it?"

"You know it is," he replied, his voice hushed. "There was no question—Derek is my brother, and we're very close. And he is, as expected, the appropriate gender for the role."

"I didn't think gender was the most important qualification." Not waiting for an answer, she moved more quickly toward their mothers, whom she'd just spotted.

"Ah, there you are, dear," her mother cooed. "We were beginning to worry." She wore a rose silk dress, the one she reserved for "occasions," and a pair of pearl earrings Marcy hadn't seen before.

"Traffic," Roger lied, clearly not wanting to continue their discussion in front of the two ladies. He saw Marcy seated, then took the place next to her.

Roger's mother smiled. "We're so glad you and Roger decided to be married at St. Michael's after all." The chic, gray-haired woman paused for a sip of water, then tilted her head. "Have you thought about the flowers yet? Our roses should be lovely that time of summer."

"Oh, that would be wonderful, wouldn't it, Marcy?" exclaimed Mrs. Winters, with a warning look that reminded her daughter of yesterday's lecture on getting off to a good start with the in-laws.

It was Marcy's turn to sip at her water while she thought of a tactful response, one that accomplished her goal but made it clear she wouldn't be steamrolled on any point, big or small. "Roses would be lovely for the altar, particularly yellow ones," she agreed, with what she hoped was a pleasing smile. "But for my bouquet, I was thinking of black-eyed Susans—they've always been my favorite."

"Black-eyed Susans for the bride's bouquet?" Mrs.

Ashforth set her water goblet down, her lips pursing into a thoughtful frown.

"Mixed with daisies, I think," Marcy added.

"How very different! I've never known anyone to do that at a wedding." The frown held, then shifted into an approving smile. "Marcy, you're such a breath of fresh air. I'm so glad you're not sticking strictly with tradition—so boring, don't you think?"

"My Marcy always did march to the beat of a different drummer," Mrs. Winters interjected. Never mind that it was a trait which generally exasperated the woman. The approval of Marcy's future mother-in-law suddenly made unconventional seem more acceptable.

Marcy exchanged a look with Roger, who seemed as surprised as she was at how well this luncheon with the mothers was going.

"Might I suggest ivory rather than white for your gown, then? I think the color tones of the flowers would be more suited to that."

"Oh, ivory is much more flattering on Marcy than white," Mrs. Winters agreed. Because it was true, Marcy nodded along with them.

"Have you considered how many attendants you'll have? I had five bridesmaids when I was married."

Roger cleared his throat. "Mother, I believe I told you already we prefer a smaller, simpler ceremony."

"Yes, yes, of course," his mother acknowledged with a dismissive wave of her hand. "Now, Roger, I know you'll ask Derek to be your best man. And your maid of honor, Marcy? Have you asked someone yet?"

Marcy drew a long breath and looked to Roger for support. He was staring at his plate.

"What about Cindy Torrence?" Marcy's mother suggested.

"Cindy? I haven't heard from her since high school graduation."

"Well, what about that lovely girl you roomed with at the university. Amanda, wasn't it?"

"Amelia, and no. I already asked Jack."

A stunned silence fell on the small group.

"I'm sorry, I must have misheard. I thought you said Jack," Mrs. Ashforth murmured.

"I did."

"Is that short for Jackie? Jacqueline?"

"Just Jack. He's been my best friend as long as I can remember."

Roger sighed. "As Mrs. Winters says, Marcy clearly marches to the beat of a different drummer."

"It *is* an unusual choice."

"Marcy, honey," her mother began in a soft tone underlaid with steely conviction, "don't you think a more traditional choice would be better? What about one of your cousins? Chrissy, or maybe Karin."

"I don't think so. We're not at all close. Besides, I believe it's traditional for the bride to ask her best friend to stand by her side at the wedding. Jack's been my best friend since third grade."

"Yes, Marcy, but—but—there are things you haven't considered. It's awkward, and Jack might not want—"

"I already asked him."

"And he agreed?" A troubled expression crossed

the older woman's face. "That does surprise me. I always thought . . . well, never mind what I thought. Marcy, Roger tells us the two of you plan to buy a house."

"We've been discussing it," Marcy agreed.

"There's a lovely place not far from us that just went on the market," Mrs. Ashforth began, then launched into a glowing description of the home's attributes. Three floors, more rooms than Marcy cared to think about cleaning, and a stable on the grounds. It sounded like the dream home of her childhood, the epitome of her dreams for her future. Although she was sure the price would be enough to make her gasp, she was equally confident it wasn't beyond the means of Roger's trust fund.

Security with a capital S.

Her fingers trembled at the thought. Uneasiness crept through her, and she couldn't say why. Maybe it was because it all seemed to be coming so easily to her and Roger. Or maybe she was afraid she wouldn't know how to behave once that secure little world was hers.

Marcy dismissed that last thought. Of course she'd know how to act. She'd act as she always had. She was herself, and aside from the general rules of politeness and civility, she was free to do as she pleased, wasn't she? Hadn't Mrs. Ashforth called her a breath of fresh air? Marcy's mother had protested Jack's part in the wedding, not Mrs. Ashforth.

As for Roger's reaction—jealousy, plain and simple. He'd never quite trusted Marcy's friendship with Jack. She hoped he'd learn to in time, because she didn't want to have to choose between them.

\* \* \*

The late afternoon sun was slanting across Jack's desk when the outer door banged open, then shut. "I could use some help out here, Jack Rathert. I saw your car, so I know you're here."

Jack grinned, recognizing the voice as much as the strident command. Sally Rose, the gray-haired virago, was his employee, not the other way around. He still jumped when she barked, though. Everyone did, and Jack credited half his success to the fact Sally Rose kept everyone on their toes and knew where everyone and everything involved in RDJ Storage Solutions was at all times.

He found her rummaging in the file room, her considerable bulk balanced on a sturdy stepladder as she pulled a box from a high shelf. "What are you looking for?"

"The specs on the last job we did for Stenson."

"That was five years ago."

"Yep, but the old man's adding more product and another warehouse. He has it in his head he needs to play with the big boys now, so he didn't even send us a bid form on the interiors."

Jack knew exactly where this was leading. "And you heard this from . . . ?"

"The warehouse foreman's wife told me at bingo."

He grinned. "I owe you another one, Sally Rose." The woman was worth her weight in gold, and that was a considerable amount.

She helped him cross-check the old specs with the information she'd garnered from her friend, then put together a rough estimate. That done, Jack called the old man's office and told his answering machine just how much money RDJ could save him.

"That ought to set his pipe glowing." Sally Rose chuckled as she sipped the coffee she'd just made for the two of them. "Now that we have that out of the way, you can tell me what you're doing here instead of fishing like you were supposed to be."

He shrugged. "Sometimes a day just doesn't turn out like you expect it to."

"Hmmph." She pulled a tablet from the jumble on his desk.

"Give me that." Jack snatched it away, irritated at the woman's nosiness. He wished she knew when to use it and when to contain it.

"Marcy Elizabeth Winters Ashforth," the old termagant recited. "I noticed you broke the lead when you crossed the last T."

"Your point?"

"Kind of has a ring to it, doesn't it? When did she get married?" Her gaze strayed to the framed picture on the wall—one of those trophy shots from the time he and Marcy had gone halibut fishing off the coast of Alaska.

"She's not married. Yet."

"But she's planning to get married, isn't she? And you're not too happy about it."

He simply arched his brows, returning her stare with one of his own. "Sally Rose, just answer one question for me, and then I want you to shut up and go home."

She looked amused. "Yes, boss?"

"What exactly does the maid of honor do?"

# TWO

When her desk phone rang, Marcy was deep into the beta release of a new spreadsheet program she'd be peddling to her corporate customers soon. Bigger, better, and more user-friendly—that's what the software company claimed, but so far Marcy couldn't get it to work.

After a moment, when the phone didn't stop, Marcy reached for it and at the same time made a mental note to talk to the office manager about the secretary who was supposed to cover the phones but never seemed to.

"Yes," she answered, her eyes still glued to the computer monitor.

"Why are you still at the office?" Jack asked in a resigned tone that indicated he already knew the answer. "The sun's shining, the wind is low, and some old geezer caught a twenty-inch trophy bass on the lee side of the lake yesterday. Didn't you see his picture on the back of the sports section?"

"What are you doing on the phone, then?" she replied with a quick glance at the wall clock. It was close to six, which explained why the secretary no longer was covering the phones.

# THE BRIDE'S BEST MAN

"The bait shop closes early on Mondays," he reminded her. "Darned shame, too, if you ask me."

"Terrible," she agreed. "They ought to stay open so you won't keep bothering hardworking people who are trying to earn a living." She shifted in her chair, rolling her shoulders to ease the ache in her back.

"Don't give me that sad song again. You already make more money than your parents ever imagined having," Jack retorted. "Why not knock off for the night and meet me for pizza? We can talk about the wedding."

The odd note in his voice worried Marcy. "You haven't changed your mind, have you? Jack, I'm counting on you. I've already told people, and I think Roger's family is starting to get used to the idea."

"I told you I would do this. That's as good as a promise, Marcy."

And Jack Rathert had never backed out on a promise. Marcy felt rotten for even suspecting he might. "Sorry. I guess I'm just a little frazzled with all that's going on. What about the wedding did you want to discuss?"

"Details like where you and what's-his-name are registered, your dress, my tux or whatever. Have you bought your dress yet?"

"Well, no, I—I haven't had time."

"You can't wait until the last minute. You have to leave time for alterations, fittings, and so forth. I'm not sure what your budget is or whether you want the traditional satin and lace or a more contemporary look, but some shops have evening hours. They all have veils, matching shoes, and that sort of thing.

We could take a quick look and narrow down the possibilities."

Marcy straightened, her aching shoulders forgotten. This couldn't be Jack talking about fittings and veils without a single snide remark thrown in. The Jack she knew had nothing but disdain for the trappings of a traditional wedding, probably because he'd long ago lost all faith in the institution of marriage.

"Have you been talking to my mother?" she finally asked him. It wouldn't be the first time the woman had tried to enlist Jack's aid in "straightening out" Marcy. He had a knack for handling Marcy's mother, but he'd never before allowed her to influence him. "Well?" she prompted when he didn't immediately answer.

"Just for a minute. On the phone."

"You called her? Why?"

"I figured she'd want to go along. She'd probably be a lot more help with the hooks and zippers, that sort of thing."

"Not from what I've heard," she replied after a moment, unable to resist the urge to tease him. She'd long ago lost count of the number of women he'd dated.

His unexpected silence threw her. She'd expected a quick comeback, and the lack of one unnerved her. "Jack, are you there?"

"Yeah," was all he said, further unnerving Marcy. Apparently she'd touched on a sore point, although she couldn't imagine why. His exploits had never been off-limits before. He'd always maintained a certain discretion, but had been the first to laugh at his

# THE BRIDE'S BEST MAN 23

own foibles and embarrassments. She wondered what had happened to change that.

As the silence stretched on the line between them, Marcy struggled for another flip remark, one that would make the previous one fade in both their memories.

Before she could think of anything, Jack cleared his throat uncomfortably. "Well, I know you didn't hear that from *my* mother." He sounded odd.

"No, actually, it was the redhead you brought to your mother's Christmas party. She was tipsy from the champagne, but fortunately she was whispering. Now about that shopping," she said, grasping for chance to change the subject back to something that in contrast seemed downright comfortable. "It was very thoughtful of you to include my mother. I know she gets on your nerves."

"Not as much as she gets on yours," he reminded her.

"True, but that's beside the point. Jack, where's all this coming from? You sound like you've been reading Martha Stewart's wedding guide."

"Not exactly. I checked around, though, to see exactly what I should be doing, and there's a lot of confusing information. I'm new to this bridesmaid thing, and I don't want to let you down."

"You won't," she assured him. "But it's not as big a deal as you're making it out to be."

"It's a big deal to me. Now back to your mother. She said you wanted an ivory gown to match the flowers you'd picked out, and that she wasn't sure you were even speaking to her."

Marcy sighed with relief. She'd stumbled with that

remark, but he'd somehow managed to right them both. "I *have* been avoiding Mom," she admitted. "She's more concerned about impressing my future in-laws than I am, and she's driving me crazy."

"She's just caught up in the excitement, plus she wants you to be happy." His voice softened. "That's what I want, too."

"I'll be happy once I get through this grand performance of a wedding my mother and Roger's are planning."

"I'll help you get through it."

A warm rush of emotion swelled in Marcy's throat. She twirled a pencil between her fingers as she fought back the unexpected tears tingling at the corners of her eyes. "With you at my side, Jack, I can get through anything, even this overblown production of a wedding."

"Good. So how's Thursday afternoon?" Jack said, his voice thick with emotion.

"For dress shopping?"

"Unless you'd rather go fishing."

She grinned ruefully at her reflection in the window glass. Typical Jack, slow to accept change but gung ho once the idea caught on. He'd been that way about fishing at first, not too interested until she'd hooked a big catfish on her own line. He'd watched her haul it in, then caught his own ten minutes later. Since then, she figured he'd spent more time fishing than sleeping.

She hadn't expected him to come around so quickly or completely this time, though. "You're serious, aren't you?"

"Absolutely. I'm going to be the best maid of

honor you ever had, although I have to admit I'm winging it."

That made her laugh outright. "It's not a contest. You don't have any competition."

"Yeah, but when there's only one shot, I figure I'd better get it right."

She smiled into the receiver. "This one's easy." She tapped the pencil, thinking a moment as she studied her calendar. "I suppose Thursday is as good a time as any. I think I can clear my calendar."

"One o'clock?"

"Make it two," she said after consulting the daybook she kept at her desk.

"Now about that pizza . . ." He let the words trail off, waiting for her answer.

"I can't. I have a new product to check out, and I can't get past the second screen. I'll see you Thursday."

"I could bring the pizza to your office."

"And blow my concentration completely? I have a better idea. Maybe this weekend we can all get together, you, me and Roger—feel free to bring a date," she offered, hoping he wouldn't reject the idea outright.

"Yeah, maybe. We'll talk about that Thursday, too." He didn't sound excited. He didn't sound upset, either. In fact, his tone carried no clue to his thoughts. Marcy sagged in her chair, wishing for an instant he was right here where she could see his expression.

"Please, I wish you'd give Roger a chance. Once you get to know him, you'll understand why I want to marry him."

Jack's voice, when he answered, betrayed the cynicism he couldn't quite hide from her. "I understand. Let's just leave it at that, OK?"

Marcy did as he suggested and dropped the subject. She only wished she could thrust it from her own mind, as well. It was still troubling her when Jack's car pulled to the curb Thursday afternoon.

"You're late," she commented as she climbed into the passenger seat. "I was beginning to think you were having second thoughts about the maid of honor thing."

He grimaced. "Do we have to keep calling it that? I'm having visions of myself in pink and lavender taffeta, and it's not a pretty sight."

"I would think not. You look terrible in lavender," she retorted with an emerging smile. Already she could feel the tension easing from her. She'd been dreading this shopping trip, but with Jack along to help ride herd on her mother, it would be all right. Cecilia adored Jack and treated him like her own son, albeit a naughty, exasperating one.

"Sorry about the time," Jack continued, looking exasperated himself. "I left early, but I forgot about the construction on the bridge. Northbound traffic is down to one lane." He signaled and maneuvered back into traffic as he spoke. "Your mother is meeting us at the store. I couldn't see any point in her driving all the way downtown to meet us."

"Ten thousand commuters thank you." A sigh escaped her as she leaned back and closed her eyes. "Where first?"

"Giselle's Wedding Warehouse."

Marcy kept her eyes closed. "I've heard of the

place," she replied diffidently. The name had a bare bones, bargain basement ring to it. Mrs. Ashforth would probably blanch at the thought of shopping there. Marcy, though, considered shopping more of a necessity than an art, so anything implying high volume and selection appealed to her. "Do they take credit cards?"

"Yep. The facilities are pretty basic compared to some of the other places I checked out, but they have a big selection, and the prices are about a third of what the big retailers charge for the same thing."

"You've already been there?" This was getting too weird.

"Better. I asked Sally Rose, and you know there's no better authority on organizing any kind of acquisition."

Having seen Sally Rose in action on more than one occasion, Marcy had to agree.

They parked two spaces away from the brown sedan that belonged to Marcy's mother, the one with the dented right front fender and the pink crocheted dream catcher hanging from the rearview mirror. Since she wasn't with the car, they assumed she was already inside.

"Care to wager which section she's in?" Jack asked as they headed for the entrance. "Mother-of-the-bride frou-frou or straight to the main program, the bridal dresses?"

"Bridal, no question about it. She can shop for herself anytime, but these days she doesn't get too many chances to pick out my clothes. She's going to be intolerable," Marcy warned.

He chuckled. "It could be worse. You could be shopping with Mama Ashforth, too."

"Wouldn't that be special," Marcy murmured. She stepped past him into the brightly lit building. Spying her mother toward the back of the store, she started toward her, only to be waylaid by a saleslady.

"May I help you? Have you been here before and filled out one of our guide sheets, or is this your first time? We have some lovely new gowns that just came in this week, and along the back wall are the most recent markdowns," she rattled on in a single breath.

"Guide sheets?" Jack murmured. "For what?"

"I'm sure my mother has already taken care of that," Marcy replied as she slid past the woman. Jack followed, looking perplexed.

"Guide sheets?" he repeated. "For what?"

"What to do when, I suppose. All that etiquette stuff. My mother's already given me two books on the subject, so I think we're covered in the reference department."

"You might have told me," he muttered.

"What?"

"Never mind. There's Cecilia." He caught Marcy's hand and tugged her toward a rack of ivory gowns.

"Goodness, your hands are cold," Marcy exclaimed.

"Nerves. All this bridal paraphernalia gives me the jitters." He ended with a grin, but Marcy could see he wasn't exactly comfortable. What man would be in this bastion of womanhood?

She wasn't exactly at ease herself. "Careful. I've heard it's contagious."

"Silk and lace?"

# THE BRIDE'S BEST MAN 29

"Wedding fever. Don't worry, though. I think you're immune."

"Thoroughly vaccinated in my youth," he agreed. "Mrs. Winters, how are you today?" he called out as they threaded their way around a prospective bride and her quarreling sisters.

"Oh, there you are. What do you think of this one, darling?" She pulled a frothy concoction of satin and lace from the rack and held it up.

Marcy glanced at the tiered layers of flounced lace and cringed inwardly. "Too much."

"I thought so, too, but I wasn't sure. You used to love those layers of lace and ruffles."

"When I was four."

"Hmm. Besides, you haven't the chest to balance all those flounces. You'd just end up looking hippy." As she spoke, she tucked that one back into place and flipped through the rack. "I already set aside several for you to try on, but we might as well pull out anything that appeals to you so we won't have to keep running back and forth." She pointed toward another rack behind her. It had wheels and a handle, and evidently was intended for that purpose.

"Let me see what you have already," Marcy decided. She rejected three outright and had her doubts about four others, but agreed to try them on to placate her mother. Then Jack offered his own find. It had a ridiculously long train and pearl-beaded panels in the skirt. The bodice, what there was of it, was heavily beaded as well. The front was cut to the navel, it seemed, and the back plunged even lower.

"I don't *think* so."

Pure devilment danced in his expression. "I'm sure you'd be lovely in it."

"I'm sure I'd catch a cold," she said, turning away with a light laugh. "Save that one for your own bride."

"On a cold day in hell."

"In that dress, it would be." She tapped her mother's arm lightly, tugging her attention away from the selection she was considering. "Mom, the rack's full. I'm going to try some of these on."

Jack hauled the rack over to the dressing rooms, then found a strategic post to lean against while he waited. "We'll be back out in a minute or two," Cecilia told him, after informing them both there were no mirrors in the dressing rooms.

Once in the dressing room, Marcy rejected two more before even zipping them up. Several more simply didn't appeal to her, and after a quick trip to the mirrors, she narrowed the selection down to two dresses. One was a simple A-line gown with pearl beading at the neckline and a lace inset in the bodice. It needed a few tucks at the waist for a better fit, but Cecilia said it was nothing she couldn't handle herself.

Jack simply shrugged his shoulders when she'd asked his opinion. "It's all right," he'd added, when pressed.

The second was one of the dresses Marcy had agreed to try on to placate her mother. It cost twice what she'd intended to spend, even here. Heaven only knew what one of the department stores would have charged for it. Besides, the train was too long.

Yet it fit her like it had been made for her, emphasizing her small breasts and tucked in waist.

Jack let out a low whistle when she stepped out of the dressing room and headed for the mirrors.

"What do you think?" she asked him as she eyed her reflection in the mirror critically. A layer of lace stitched with seed pearls covered the high-necked bodice and sleeves. The dual-layered skirt was mist floating above satin, smooth and cut on the bias so it draped beautifully over her full hips, slimming and shaping, hiding and revealing.

Jack never answered. After a moment, Marcy turned around. "Well?" she prompted.

He simply stared back at her, oddly solemn.

"Jack?"

"That's the dress," he said at last. He cleared his throat and grinned. "If you have to get married, you might as well do it in a dress that makes you look like a fairy princess come to life."

"A fairy princess, huh?" Marcy studied her reflection in the mirror. The dress was beautiful. In it, she looked beautiful, too. A beautiful stranger.

It was an unsettling feeling, and suddenly this all seemed very real. All the talk, all the plans until now had been just that, talk and plans. Now, at this moment in this dress, she felt the full impact of the decision she'd made.

Her life was about to change, probably in ways she couldn't even guess at. She would leave her familiar world and enter a new one as different from the way she'd grown up as winter differed from summer. Could she make the leap? Was she clever enough to transform herself from simple Marcy Winters to Mrs.

Roger Ashforth? Could she fit in without losing herself in the process?

"Well, dear, what do you think?"

Marcy blinked, then focused her eyes on her mother's reflection standing next to hers. "About what?"

Her mother looked away from the mirror, her expression an odd mixture of satisfaction and amusement. "About the dress, of course. Quit daydreaming."

"It is nice, but—" Marcy began.

"You'll only get married once. It should be perfect—and you have to admit that dress is as close to perfect as anything we've seen so far," her mother pronounced with such certainty that Marcy took another look in the mirror. "Isn't that right, Jack?"

"Any closer and we'd have to have her bronzed." His voice sounded thick, lower than usual and kind of gravelly. He cleared his throat, then coughed. "Just get the dress. We'll call it a day and get some dinner," he urged.

"Yeah," she murmured, turning back to the mirror. The dress was perfect. She was the one with the flaws.

A tiny finger of fear clawed from her gut into her throat. She'd spent her adult years searching for the right man, the perfect complement to her ambitions, the one who would fit the role she'd envisioned in her perfect future. She hadn't considered how she'd fit his vision until now.

\* \* \*

Jack dreamed of the northern wilderness that night, of clean air, miles and miles of untouched forests, and a high mountain lake filled with the best-tasting grayling on Earth. He recognized the place immediately. He'd been there last summer and he planned to go back again and again.

At first he dreamed he was night fishing from the shore. Although the fishing was going well, something didn't seem quite right, so he piled his gear into the small johnboat and rowed to the middle of the lake. He fished for a while, catching some and letting them go because he just didn't feel like keeping them. He'd just thrown out his line again when he heard movement behind him.

Glancing back, he saw Marcy in the boat with him. She cast her line into the lake and smiled. Feeling better now that she'd joined him, Jack smiled back, then returned to his fishing. A big grayling splashed close to the boat. "Did you see that?" he called softly to Marcy, but she didn't answer. When he turned around, she was gone.

The grayling splashed again. Jack looked toward the ripples, but it was Marcy in the lake. She rose up out of the water, her face illuminated by the moonlight, her body hidden by the rising mist. The mist swirled and settled, revealing the ivory wedding dress. It glimmered in the moonlight, absorbing the light, then radiating it with a power source all its own.

"Marcy?" he called out.

She beckoned him to follow, but he discovered the oars had disappeared. He searched the boat, then the water, and finally leaned over the edge and tried to hand paddle his way toward her.

She shook her head sadly and beckoned once more. She waited only a moment, then slowly walked across the water toward the shore. She looked back once from the shore before she disappeared into the trees. Then a cloud passed over the moon, and he couldn't even see the trees.

Frantic now, he leaned toward the water and began to splash. A fish leaped into the air, close enough to touch, then hovered an instant. "Idiot!" it said in a voice like his father's. The fish spit cold lake water into Jack's face.

He awoke with a harsh jerk, knocking the lamp from the bedside table. While one part of his brain registered the crash and accompanying pop of the bulb breaking in the socket, the rest tried to shake off the eerie, disoriented feeling left by the dream. He sat there a moment, breathing hard, chilled by the icy sweat covering his body. He'd had weird dreams before, odd permutations of the day's events. Usually it meant he'd had too much chili for dinner or was obsessing about a particular project and needed to ease off.

Maybe that's what this was. He was too obsessed with being the best maid of honor a guy could be. Maybe it didn't have to be the big deal he was making of it. That's why he'd dreamed about Marcy walking away from him—on water, no less—and why his father had spoken through a fish, then spit on him. He let that thought simmer for a moment, but it didn't clear his mind any. After a bit, he eased himself off the edge of the bed opposite the lamp and closed the window.

He grabbed his robe and shuffled toward the light

switch to survey the damage. By the time he'd cleaned that up, then warmed himself with a hot shower and a cup of cocoa, he figured the dream had faded enough that he could safely go back to sleep.

He did, eventually, and if he dreamed anything else he didn't remember it. It was a good thing, too, because he found he had enough trouble pushing the image of Marcy's sad eyes and that glowing dress from his mind.

The spitting fish didn't exactly fade away, either, he decided several days later as he stared down at the menu at Café LaRosa. It seemed to be nothing but fish and things he couldn't pronounce, let alone identify. He should have expected as much, considering the fact Roger Ashforth was hosting this little get-together.

"Jack, you like fish, don't you? The salmon here is excellent," Roger said from his seat opposite Jack. Marcy sat to Roger's right, and three others filled out the rest of the table, including a married couple consisting of Roger's best friend and his wife, who happened to be Roger's stockbroker as well. The other guest was the stockbroker's sister, who was visiting for a few days.

"Yes, and the dill sauce is incomparable," the stockbroker agreed. Ingrid, he thought her name was. She had a taut, nervous smile, and the smoke from her cigarette blew directly into Jack's eyes.

"Hmm. I'm sure. I think, though, I'll have the prime rib for a change," Jack replied. He'd lost his taste for fish lately, although he figured that was a temporary thing. He casually leaned back in his chair, hoping to escape the smoke's path. He caught Marcy's apologetic gaze and forced a smile.

"How's business, Roger?" Jack asked.

"Fine, fine. I have an interesting deal pending, but I really can't talk about it until everything is settled," Roger answered with a dismissive smile. "Everything all right on your end of the street?"

"Couldn't be better," Jack said, meeting one nonanswer with another.

"Roger tells me you have your own business—furniture or something like that, isn't it?" The query came from Sonia, Ingrid's sister.

"Commercial cabinetry," he answered, studying her. She looked expensive, the epitome of good taste and breeding from the top of her two-hundred-dollar haircut to the tips of her kid leather shoes.

Her carefully tweaked eyebrows arched with interest. "That sounds profitable, considering the building boom around here. Did you establish the company yourself or did you inherit?"

"My father was a carpenter. I just expanded on what he'd established."

"Marcy, he's being modest, isn't he?" Sonia's gaze slid sideways, then back to Jack's face. "I think the most interesting people are those who have made their own way." Mischief glittered in her aqua blue eyes, and he wondered briefly if the color was a gift of nature or an accessory to her outfit. The stroke of her foot across his shoe and up his ankle drove the thought from his mind.

"Really?" He sat perfectly still, unsure what to do, unsure what he wanted to do. He didn't even know the woman, and already she was seducing him beneath the table. Occasionally, under the right circumstances, he enjoyed that kind of game. Right now it left him unsettled.

"Sonia has her own public relations firm. She's been talking with Roger this evening about some ideas she has for Ashforth Industries," Marcy explained in her best hostess voice. Jack recognized the tone. It was the same one Marcy had used when she introduced him to an out-of-town cousin she didn't like but was forced to entertain.

"Ah, a fellow entrepreneur," he commented as he withdrew his leg. Sonia gave a little wink and turned to Roger with a question about the menu. Her long lashes fluttered prettily, and she released a tinkling laugh over something Roger had said too low for Jack to hear.

"I hate to bring up business now," she continued a little louder now, "but I just thought of something. Do you recall the campaign for the Home Builders Association a few years ago?" Once again, her voice dipped lower, and Jack found it difficult to make out more than the odd word amidst the background noise of the restaurant.

Jack glanced back at Marcy, who betrayed her irritation with a faint flutter of her fingertips before responding to a comment from one of the others. Then he felt Sonia's touch again. This time she'd taken off her shoe and was running a stockinged toe up his calf. Once more, he moved away.

It was going to be a long, strange evening.

The waiter's arrival provided a momentary respite. While the others ordered, Jack found himself studying Roger and Marcy. Something was amiss. It was apparent in the stiff set of Marcy's shoulders and in the way she held herself apart from Roger. Roger, too, seemed distant. Last time Jack had seen them together, they'd been constantly touching—on the shoulder, the arm, or just holding hands.

An argument on the way here, Jack guessed, taking heart. Maybe there was trouble in paradise. Maybe he wouldn't lose his best buddy after all. Certainly something was brewing.

As Roger leaned toward Sonia, laughing with her, Jack saw a flicker of hurt in Marcy's expression before she masked it.

The observation triggered a pang of guilt. He shouldn't be so selfish. A true friend would put Marcy's happiness first, even if it meant their friendship would change. So what? Change was inevitable, and the process had begun long before Marcy had announced her engagement. It would continue whether he acted in her best interests or not.

Sonia laughed again, drawing his gaze to the hand she'd laid lightly on Roger's sleeve. Marcy didn't respond, but she noticed, too. Jack could tell by the tight set of her lips as she listened to Ingrid's husband's suggestions for the reception. Knowing Marcy as he did, Jack guessed Roger would catch hell for the little game he was playing with Sonia, but not until they were alone. Ingrid noticed, too, and she shot her sister a stern look. Sonia merely smiled, a wide, cat-trapping-the-mouse grin.

Jack's own lips thinned, and he reached for his water glass. Seconds later water splashed, and Sonia emitted a shocked gasp and leaped to her feet, knocking over the chair behind her.

# THE BRIDE'S BEST MAN

"Sorry, damned clumsy of me," Jack exclaimed, half standing as he snatched at napkins. He passed three to her and dabbed at the water spots on the front of her dress to further distract her. To her credit, after the initial shock wore off, she handled herself with amused dignity.

Catching his hand with one of her own, she extracted the napkin from him and smiled thinly. "I think I can handle it from here. If you'll all excuse me for a few moments, I'll see if I can find the ladies' room and freshen up."

"Would you like some help?" Marcy offered, sounding solicitous. Shushing the other woman's protest with a technique worthy of Roger's mother, Marcy took Sonia's arm and led the way through the tables toward the restaurant's rear wall.

If Jack hadn't known her so well, he'd have missed the flicker of gratitude in her eyes when her gaze settled briefly on him as she'd turned away. As it was, he had to stifle a grin. They made a good team. He'd created the opportunity, and he had no doubt she was now setting Sonia straight on a few key points.

While Roger summoned a waiter to set the table to rights, Jack made a show of expressing his regrets over his clumsiness.

By the time the two women returned, the table had been freshly laid and Jack had taken Sonia's seat. "I'm a lefty. With Ingrid's sister being right-handed, I thought the switch might prevent any further accidents," he explained.

"Hmm, I never realized you were left-handed," Roger commented.

Marcy's lips twitched, but she didn't say a word.

When she took her seat, though, he noticed she seemed less tense than before. Sonia seemed to have lost none of her sauciness, which made him wonder exactly what had transpired out of his earshot.

"Marcy, I do admire you for bucking tradition and picking this gorgeous man for your attendant. So twenty-first century, don't you think?" Sonia finished, nodding toward her sister. "And we thought we were rebelling by eloping."

Jack's gaze immediately dropped to her left hand, and she smiled silkily. "Divorced last year. The rebellion was a kick. The marriage wasn't. Keep that in mind, Marcy."

"Rebellion has nothing to do with it," Marcy explained. "Jack and I grew up together. He's the best friend anyone could ever have, practically my brother."

At her words, Jack felt the same clench in his guts he'd experienced when she'd walked out of the dressing room at Giselle's Wedding Warehouse wearing that lace and mist dress.

Again in his mind's eye, he saw her at the mirror, her eyes uncertain, her cheeks flushed. Then the image shifted into the lakeside one of her with the dress aglow. Shaking his head slightly, he wished he could erase both pictures from his thoughts. Otherwise, he might not make it through the next few weeks with his mind intact.

"How touching, don't you think, Roger? You're comfortable with this, I take it."

"Why wouldn't I be? Jack's a great guy. I'm looking forward to getting to know him better." The words were right, but his eyes carried a different sentiment—resentment, Jack noted, unless he'd misread the man. That didn't bode well for the future of his and Marcy's friendship.

Jack wasn't sure how he made it through the rest of the evening. Practiced charm and luck, he supposed, plus a knack for small talk. It helped that Sonia behaved herself after his stunt with the water, although she still managed a few barbed remarks toward Marcy and continued to flirt with Roger. Finally, though, Jack was alone in his car, driving toward home.

He couldn't wait to get there. He'd already shed his tie, and as soon as he walked through the door, he'd shed these new leather loafers and linen trousers in favor of old socks and sweatpants. Then he'd kick back in the recliner and watch the end of the baseball game. Or maybe he'd go straight to the new fishing gear catalog and see whether the company still carried those multipocketed sports vests. The one Marcy had given him for his birthday several years ago was worn beyond patching.

Marcy.

Suddenly he didn't feel much like going home to the game and the catalog. At the next exit, he turned the car back around and headed toward the paperwork he'd left on his desk at the office. If he was going to mope and stew over Marcy's choices, he might as well get some work done at the same time. Maybe then he'd have a little something good to offset the rotten feeling in the pit of his stomach.

An hour later, though, he found himself staring at the computer screen with nothing more accomplished than when he'd arrived. Giving up the pretense, he shoved back his chair.

There was no question what was bothering him. He didn't want Marcy to marry Roger Ashforth. A few days ago, he'd thought it inevitable, that he simply needed time to get used to the idea. Now he wasn't so sure.

Marcy had been miserable tonight, and although she'd evidently set Sonia straight, Jack could see a lifetime's worth of women like Sonia in Marcy's future if she married Roger.

A real friend cared enough to do what was right, and Jack knew the right thing to do was to stop this wedding. He'd have to be careful, though. Somehow, he'd have to make Marcy think it was her idea. Otherwise, she might end up hating him.

The thought was a sobering one. She might hate him anyway, but as painful as that would be, the idea of her marrying Roger hurt worse. He decided to risk it.

He'd have to be subtle, though, more careful than he'd ever been. Otherwise, the plan was doomed to failure.

He stopped short. Plan? What plan?

# THREE

The flowers arrived by special messenger as Marcy was returning from a meeting. "For you, Ms. Winters," the department secretary called out as Marcy hurried past. "He says he needs your signature."

"For flowers? That's odd."

"For this," the messenger said, handing her a large envelope.

"OK." Still puzzled, she signed the sheet on the clipboard he held out, then cleared a place on the corner of her desk for the vase.

"I guess Mr. Ashforth got tired of sending roses," the secretary said as she leaned close to sniff the arrangement of lupines, daisies, black-eyed Susans, columbines, and wild-looking ferns—all her favorites clustered together in a single arrangement. A comforting warmth suffused her. He'd remembered her favorites and taken time to order them instead of the florist's standard offering.

It was the best apology she'd ever received. All her anger over last night's disagreement, over the way he'd needled her and flirted with Sonia, faded away.

"There's a card." The secretary plucked it from the holder and handed it to Marcy. "Something short, sweet, and sappy, I'll bet. Some women have all the luck."

"I suppose I am lucky," Marcy murmured. A handsome, wealthy fiancé who certainly knew how to tailor an apology to the tastes of the woman he loved. She slipped the card from its miniature envelope, knowing her relief shone in a silly, sappy smile and not caring it would be the subject of office gossip the rest of the afternoon.

The disagreement before dinner had been unpleasant, but after had been worse. She'd ranted like a jealous shrew, and Roger had retreated into an unduly dignified silence. Just the memory caused a tremor of unease, and she shoved the feeling away. It wasn't their first disagreement, and it certainly wouldn't be their last.

Roger's gesture overshadowed the lingering hurt over his flirting. Flowers, she decided, made an excellent apology.

Her smile froze as she read the scrawled message on the card—a message *not* penned in Roger's neat handwriting.

*For the altar? Or something bigger? Sunflowers? The florist said she'd be able to get some flown in even though they'll be out of season by the wedding date.*
*Jack*

Jack? Sunflowers for the altar?

Feeling disoriented, Marcy slit open the large envelope. The sheaf of papers inside consisted of price sheets, photos, and several pages of testimonials, courtesy of the florist who'd arranged the flowers.

"Damn!" Marcy's gaze swiveled from the card to the flowers and back again. The warmth she'd felt at the sight of the arrangement faded into disappointment and anger.

"Is something wrong, Ms. Winters?"

Marcy forced a smile to her lips as she glanced up at the secretary. "No, nothing really. I just remembered something I need to do."

"Anything I can help with?"

"No, but thank you anyway."

She waited until the door clicked closed behind the secretary before she flopped disconsolately into her chair. Damn, damn, and double damn! There was something she needed to do, all right. She needed to give Roger a good piece of her mind. She needed to—

No, she was the one who needed her head examined. This intense disappointment was her doing, not Roger's. She should have remembered he never sent anything but roses. That was simply his style— classy and sophisticated. Comfortably predictable. *Perfect blossoms for the perfect lady*, he'd said the first time he'd brought her roses, and he'd never sent any other kind of flower.

Not exactly an original sentiment, but one that made her feel treasured just the same. That's what she needed, someone steady and dependable, a partner with the same desire for family and fidelity and the capacity to provide both.

Maybe the roses would arrive later. Maybe Roger would bring them himself when he picked her up tonight. Maybe she should surprise *him* with roses instead.

She'd been as much to blame for their disagreement as he had. Granted, she hadn't exacerbated the situation by flirting with someone else, but considering her choice of wedding attendants, maybe Roger had reason to view the situation differently. Maybe he wasn't as secure about their relationship as she'd thought.

She picked up the phone and dialed Roger's office. He wasn't in, and she didn't feel like leaving a message. What would she say, *I'm thinking of you and wishing you'd sent the flowers instead of Jack?*

She dialed Jack's number instead. Sally Rose recognized Marcy's voice immediately. "He just walked in, and he's wearing a frown that would scare a grizzly bear. See if you can't put him in a better mood before I have to deal with him, please."

"Something wrong?" she asked when Jack growled into the phone.

"Marcy!" A note of pleasure replaced the growl. "You got my message?"

"If it came in a vase, yes, I did. I can't believe you're vetting florists for me or are you just trying to make brownie points with some cute little blond in the shop?"

"I do something nice for my best friend, and this is the thanks I get?"

"You do have a certain history."

"Maybe, but this time I'm innocent."

"I'll settle for not guilty. You were never innocent."

His low laugh brought a smile to her lips. "I was checking on a job downtown and spotted them in the window of a florist's shop. They reminded me of

# THE BRIDE'S BEST MAN 47

you. Black-eyed Susans are still your favorites, aren't they?"

"Of course, although I do have a weakness for those wild roses that grow along the bank of Miller Creek."

"Mmm. The sweet smell of summer. I don't know about the wild roses, but the woman at the florist's shop said she'd be able to have anything in that vase flown in even though they'll probably all be out of season by the time the wedding gets here."

Marcy shook her head, nonplussed at his enthusiasm. The dress-shopping trip had been surprise enough, but she thought that would cure him of this odd enthusiasm for the traditional maid of honor duties. Obviously she was wrong. He was taking this seriously, much too seriously.

"Jack, you really didn't have to go to so much trouble, although I do appreciate your sending this. It's been a difficult day, and my office could use some brightening."

"Just trying to do the job you asked me to do, ma'am. Besides, it wasn't out of my way, I had the time, and the shop's owner was charming."

"I knew there had to be a blond involved in this."

"Not a blond, although she may have been twenty years ago."

"Meaning?"

"Meaning I'm hurt at your lack of faith in me. I put a sweet and talented gray-haired grandmother in touch with my best friend, who happens to be in need of the dear lady's unique skills, and all I get is grief."

Despite the exaggerated pain in his voice, Marcy heard the amusement underneath.

"Yes, well sweet old ladies often have beautiful, nubile daughters. And granddaughters."

"Nope. Single, childless, but with one nephew whose brood of boys seems to fill the gap for her. She showed me the pictures."

"Don't they always?" No wonder Jack didn't feel the need for a home and family of his own. His infallible charm brought out the mothering instincts of every woman over the age of fifty and the sweltering hormones of those younger. He had all the benefits with none of the responsibilities.

"Anyway, speaking of family ties," he continued, "I'm driving home tonight. It's Rose Festival weekend. How about you? We could carpool."

"Thanks for the offer, but I'm tied up tonight."

"Really? I've underestimated Roger. Handcuffs or soft cotton rope?"

"What are you—oh, knock it off," she chided as his teasing laughter rumbled in her ear.

"You used to be a lot quicker than that. Not sleeping well? Not a surprise, considering the handcuffs."

"How adolescent," she replied. "Some of Roger's business associates are giving a party at the Plaza Rooftop. We're driving down tomorrow to take Mother out for lunch. It's her birthday."

A low whistle sounded in her ear. "Impressive. You gonna wear that little off-the-shoulder number?"

"To my mother's birthday lunch?"

"Don't be obtuse. Tonight."

"Maybe. Why?"

"Just remembering."

"Remembering what?"

"How you looked in it at the Gellmans' party."

"I'm surprised you noticed. You were with the dancer that night, weren't you? Or was it the dental assistant?"

"I always notice you."

"Really? And what color is the beading at the hemline of that dress."

"Burgundy with a thin line of gold. Same thing along the lace section in the front, and there are roses in the lace, some fully open and some just rosebuds."

A tremor crept up Marcy's spine. She wasn't sure when the tone of this conversation had changed, just that it had. He wasn't teasing her anymore. She wasn't sure what he was doing, only that his tone had turned serious. Intense.

"At the Gellmans' party, you wore a thin, herringbone patterned gold chain around your neck. Your earrings were gold knots with a ruby and two diamonds in each—a birthday gift from Roger, I think," he continued. "Last year at the mayor's house you wore a pair of simple gold hoops and the same dress. I preferred the gold hoops. They suit you better than the glitter."

Marcy's breath caught in surprise. A silence stretched between them, fragile as the stillness on a snowdrifted mountain. The tremor extended to her limbs, and she sank into her chair. "I don't know what to say," she answered at last.

"Sometimes I don't either," he replied enigmatically.

\* \* \*

The details. That's how Jack had done it, Marcy decided the next morning as she wandered the path in her mother's rose garden. He'd recited an unexpected list of details, the type of things men don't usually notice or remember, then taken it one step further. He'd made it intensely personal.

Too bad she couldn't throw the two men into a big blender and combine them into one. Roger's sense of family loyalty, his ambition, and his marital goals plus Jack's sense of fun. She'd have the perfect man. The idea lingered.

It had clung like a cocklebur through the evening's party, no matter how she tried to shake it off. It didn't help that Roger's father had pleaded business concerns and sent his son off to London before the party had finished. Roger had murmured an apology, then caught a cab, leaving her to make the drive home alone—home to her apartment, and, this morning, home to Bridgeton.

Sinking onto a bench tucked into a corner of the garden, she closed her eyes and concentrated on the sweet scent of the roses mingled with the smell of fresh-mown grass. The sounds of small-town life filled her ears—a lawn mower a few houses away, the slam of a screen door behind raucous children, and, in the distance, the toots and blasts of the high school band warming up for the Rose Festival parade.

It wasn't enough to distract her from her thoughts, though. For the first time she could remember, Marcy caught herself wishing her mother would hurry up and join her.

Cecilia, being Cecilia, didn't disappoint her daughter on that count. "There you are, dear," she called out the back door, just seconds later. "We should hurry. I'm already ten minutes late for my shift at the ladies' auxiliary booth."

Marcy started toward her. "My purse is already in the car."

"Oh, we'll never find a parking space. You remember what it's like along the parade route. No, we might as well walk, don't you think?" Cecilia pulled the door closed and checked the lock.

"I thought you were late."

"Another ten minutes won't make that much difference. Too bad you couldn't ride with Jack and save on gasoline," Cecilia muttered as they passed the Rathert's empty driveway. "He and Lizzy left early, before I even had my shower. I never did understand why Lizzy always had to be up and about before the crack of dawn."

Cecilia chattered the entire ten blocks, updating Marcy on the Feldmans' divorce, the newest Wilson child, and a dozen other tidbits of local news. Marcy could scarcely get a word in edgewise before her excited mother launched into the next story.

Lizzy spotted them before they reached the booth. "Marcy, child, it's about time!" she called out as she hurried forward. "When Jack said you were bringing your fiancé down to meet everyone, I was so excited. Now, where is that handsome young man? Sidetracked at the shooting gallery already? I told Cecelia to take the long way around or that would happen." Her ample arms folded Marcy into a warm hug.

"Roger's in London," Marcy answered as she returned the hug, then explained while the three of them made their way to the back of the booth.

"That's too bad. I was looking forward to checking him out to see whether he's everything Cecilia said," Lizzie teased as she bent to finish unpacking a box of coffee mugs for the booth's display.

"Well, I think it's good he's getting these problems settled now so he won't have to travel much after they're married."

Lizziy winked and continued unpacking. "Your mother's a bit naive about these things, but having been married to a so-called businessman—"

"Knock it off, Mom." Jack stepped around the curtain at the back of the booth, his arms loaded with two more boxes.

"I was just saying that—"

"Well, don't," he interrupted, his tone mild, but his eyes flashing a warning as he eased the boxes onto the ground next to the others. "The situation is completely different. I've met Roger. While he's not exactly the man I would have picked for Marcy, she could have done a lot worse."

Marcy smiled thinly. "Thank you—I think."

He straightened, rubbing his chin as he glanced around. "So where is the white knight, anyway?"

"In London. Business," she replied shortly.

He released an exaggerated sigh. "Then I suppose it's up to me to fight the dragons for you, fair lady." He caught her hand, tugging her toward the booth's back exit.

"What dragons?"

"You go along now and have fun while you still

# THE BRIDE'S BEST MAN

can," Cecilia said with a gentle nudge. "Lizzy and I have everything under control here."

"One thing, Jack," Lizzy called after them.

"Yes, Mother?"

"Feed the girl something. She's thin as a stray cat."

"And just as prickly," he added quietly.

Marcy snatched her hand out of his grasp and stalked after him. "Just what's that supposed to mean?"

"You look edgy, that's all."

"I'm tired."

"Nope. When you're tired, you get purple shadows under your eyes. You're distracted, you walk slow, and you don't rise to the bait much."

She cast a suspicious look sideways. "And you're baiting me?"

"Maybe. Want a brownie?" he asked, stopping at a baked goods booth sponsored by one of the town's church groups.

"All that sugar will probably make me more edgy," she snapped back as she selected a thick, fudgy wedge with caramel swirls in the topping. "How about a shooting match to work it off?" She started in that direction, leaving him to pay for the brownies and catch up.

By the time he'd reached the shooting gallery, she'd already paid for both of them and chosen her weapon. "Two out of three?" she challenged.

"Not fair. You know this isn't my game."

"Does this mean you're not up to the challenge?"

He picked up the sideshow gallery rifle next to hers and leaned on the counter, his elbow brushing against hers. "Two games out of three here, two out of three at the ring toss, same at hoop fishing."

"Winner buys the hot fudge sundaes," she agreed. "Top row, third from the corner." She took aim at the whirling target, concentrated, and fired.

"Got it! Beat that, buddy."

He drew in a deep breath and aimed. "What do you think, the grinning fox on the third row, or the lion on the second?"

"You're asking me?" She leaned toward him, pretending to peer through the sights from her position at his shoulder. "I think you'd better go for the elephant. Bigger target."

"I'll take the fox."

He missed.

"It's in the bag," she taunted, then called out her target and aimed. Her finger pulled at the trigger, and Jack bumped her elbow. The shot went wide, pinging the booth's roof.

She jabbed hard with her own elbow. "Cheat!"

"Just evening the odds," he replied, taking her jab with a mild grunt as he aimed his own gallery gun.

She blew in his ear. His shot pinged the booth operator on the shoulder. The youth yelped and ducked under the counter.

"Don't do that unless you mean business," Jack grumbled, his voice harsh.

Marcy noticed a flush rising on his neck and grinned. "Hot fudge sundaes are serious business."

"That wasn't the kind of business I meant." He winked, then took his next shot while she was still wondering at his low, sultry tone. "Next time you blow in my ear, make sure we're someplace private."

# THE BRIDE'S BEST MAN 55

"In your dreams, buddy," she returned, nudging him to throw off his next shot.

The battle escalated from there. He tickled her. She bumped him. Neither won—at anything.

It didn't matter. The good-natured tussling chased away the unsettled feeling that had been haunting her. "OK, truce," she offered finally. "I'll buy the sundaes."

"Which is only right, since you cheated."

"Just me?"

"All's fair in love and war," he reminded her.

Her gaze slid away from his as the unsettled feeling returned. Love and war.

"Look, stained glass!" She pointed to the next booth. She hurried through the crowd to the display and studied the hanging pieces. Some of the larger ones were magnificent, but the smaller ones drew her. Little ones could fit anywhere. They needed only a suction cup with a hook to attach to any window, so they could easily make the move from her apartment to wherever she ended up.

"I think I'll get the hummingbird."

"No surprise there. Your mother still keeps a feeder, doesn't she?"

"I think so." She hadn't noticed this morning with her mind otherwise occupied. She paid for the purchase and tucked it into her shoulder bag.

"I suppose we should head back toward the mothers, don't you think?" she said after they'd wandered among the booths for a bit longer.

Jack looked up from the carved walking stick he was examining. "Maybe." He set it aside, then hesitated. "You know, I'm going to miss you."

"What do you mean?"

He stepped closer, his expression serious. "This is it, the last time we'll do this. After you get married, you won't be horsing around with me, blowing in my ear to throw off my aim, or just hanging out."

"It doesn't have to be that way."

"It's just how things work. You'll be busy in your new life. You'll move on, and after a while we'll get together twice a year, maybe three times, send Christmas cards, call once in a while." He caught a lock of her hair in one hand and slowly stroked its length, his gaze flickering between it and her. She couldn't look away from the sadness in his eyes. "I'll miss this," he repeated, then released her hair.

"So you've decided to abandon me?" she answered.

A slow smile transformed his face back into the visage she knew so well. "Not quite yet. Let's get those sundaes."

They'd almost made it back to the refreshment booths when Marcy spotted the painting. The artist had to be local, although she recognized neither the signature nor the woman running the booth. The scene, however, she knew well. "Miller Creek," she murmured, leaning closer to study the painting.

The artist had captured it perfectly, the overgrown, arching clusters of multiflora rosebushes dotting the banks and the fallen petals floating on the water's surface. Just a hint of morning mist rose above the water, which looked as inviting as any June day she could remember at the place. It had been their spot, hers and Jack's, from the time they'd been old enough to slip away on their own to fish or just dangle their bare feet at the creek's edge.

"Ink and watercolor. Simply amazing," Marcy exclaimed. "I wish I could do this, but since I can't, I'll just have to buy it."

"It's already sold," Jack said, drawing her attention to the marker hung over the corner of the frame. "Too bad."

"Hello, Jack," the booth operator exclaimed as she came up beside them. "Come to pick up your painting?"

He shifted uncomfortably, and Marcy eyed him with suspicion. "You bought this?"

"First thing this morning," the other woman confirmed. "Your Jack's quite the early bird. Should I wrap it now?"

Jack hesitated, then nodded. "Please."

"You weren't going to tell me!"

Resignation replaced his smile, and he released a loud sigh. "If you must know, I bought it for you. A wedding present. So you wouldn't forget where you came from and know you can always come back and still belong."

Marcy stood perfectly still. She couldn't have spoken even if she wanted to. In truth, she had no words—and no voice, either, thanks to the lump forming in her throat. Instead, she leaned close and kissed Jack's cheek.

"Thank you," she managed at last. "You're the very best friend anyone could ever have."

He didn't quite smile, but there was a hint of mistiness in his eyes, much like Marcy's own. "I guess I'll have to settle for that," he said.

* * *

"What do you think of the wine?" Jack's mother, Lizzy, refilled the cup Marcy had placed on a shelf beneath the counter at the refreshment stand while she tended to a customer.

"It's good, Lizzy. Is it local?"

"From that little place just outside of town."

Nearby, the band eased from a slow waltz into the more lively beat of a polka with barely a pause. Marcy glanced up from her vantage point behind the refreshment counter and grinned as she spotted her mother dancing with Ed Rappaport, who'd been Marcy's high school history teacher.

Then Jack moved into view with his partner, Jennifer Parker, who'd graduated a year behind Marcy and Jack. She'd heard about Jennifer's divorce and her ex-husband's bankruptcy. Right now the woman looked like she'd be happy to console herself with Jack. Marcy hoped Jack recognized that sickeningly sweet smile for what it was.

Lizzy nudged her elbow and winked. "Cute, aren't they? For an old guy, he's not half bad, if you like the aging fraternity man type. You know, Ed's wife has been dead five years now."

*Cute? Aging fraternity man?* It took Marcy a few seconds to realize Lizzy wasn't talking about her son and Jennifer Parker. "Mom and Mr. Rappaport?"

Lizzy nodded, her expression unreadable.

"If you're trying to tell me something, just come out and say it."

"It's not for me to say."

"You brought it up."

Lizzy's dramatic sigh signaled a forthcoming revelation. Marcy finished with the customer she was helping, then followed Lizzy to a corner where they wouldn't be heard. "Well?"

Lizzy pretended reluctance, but Marcy knew her well enough to suspect the woman had been aching for such an opportunity. "Go on. Spill it," Marcy urged.

A shrug lifted Lizzy's shoulders, and she sighed again. "They've been seeing each other a bit. All library committee work, of course. Nothing outright serious, but I think he's sweet on her."

"Mother would have told you if something was going on between them."

"True, but you know Cecilia." The back door to the refreshment stand squeaked open, then closed, and Lizzy lowered her voice to a whisper. "She can't see the forest for the trees." Her gaze slid past Marcy, and her expression shifted into what she called her social face. "Ed, I didn't see your name on the volunteers list for tonight," she said loudly.

"It's not," he answered, barely glancing at Lizzy. "Hello, there, Miss Marcy. You know how to polka, don't you?" Ed caught her by the hand and tugged her toward the exit.

"Yes, I do, but I can't abandon Lizzy and the others."

"Why not? Don't you worry about me," Lizzy said. "We'll talk tomorrow."

Sensing Marcy's hesitation, Ed tilted his head and grinned. "What's the matter? Afraid you can't keep up with this old man?" He leaned close and delivered a broad wink. "You're supposed to be checking me out, and so far you're falling down on the job."

"I really don't know what—"

"Watch it, Marcy. You don't lie any better now than when you were fourteen years old. Come on now, and you can tell me the way to your mother's heart."

Bemused, Marcy followed. "Mr. Rappaport, I'm a little confused. Mother hasn't said anything about you."

"High school's over. Call me Ed," he ordered as he stepped onto the dance floor, pulling Marcy along with the lively beat. Her feet soon found the rhythm as Ed guided her through the steps.

From the corner of her eye, she spotted Jack. He stood at the far side of the dance floor, scanning the crowd. Then Ed spun her around, and she lost sight of him. By the time they'd turned again, Jack had disappeared.

"So is Lizzy right?" Marcy asked. "Do you have a thing for Mother?"

"Absolutely. Ceci is a very special, very good-hearted woman."

"Ceci?"

"Your mother, of course." He executed another careful turn around a more exuberant couple, sparing them all a spill off the edge of the dance floor.

"Of course." Marcy grinned wryly. "I'd never heard her called that."

"Cecilia's too stuffy for such a sweet, fun lady, don't you think? Look at her now," he turned his head, and Marcy followed the direction of his gaze. Cecilia was with Jack, and Jennifer Parker was nowhere to be seen.

"You have a point," Marcy agreed. She caught several glimpses of her mother dancing with Jack as Ed maneuvered them closer. Cecilia seemed more animated than usual. Her eyes danced with excitement, and her hair was styled differently, making her look younger.

"Do you have any objections to my seeing your mother? Formally, I mean. Dating."

She tried to look thoughtful, but she couldn't contain her amusement. "Why are you asking me?"

"Just hedging my bets. I haven't asked her yet, but I did think since you were here in town, I might as well see what I'm up against."

She had to look away. "This is too weird," she finally said. "This isn't the 1950s, and I'm not in charge of her virtue."

"No, but you could stand in my way if you didn't like the idea," he explained. "I prefer to state my intentions clearly—and they are serious. I've been alone for some time now, and I think I deserve another chance at happiness."

Marcy stared him squarely in the eyes. "Go for it, then."

She'd never seen the man grin so broadly. "Thank you, Marcy. Switch partners, then," he called out. Without missing a step, he twirled her away, and she landed in Jack's arms.

Marcy blinked her confusion, and stared up at Jack as she regained her rhythm. "Well, that was different."

"I'm not sure what that was." He glanced sideways at the older couple and shook his head, as confused as Marcy.

"Young love brewing," she explained. "He just asked for my blessing."

"Mr. Rappaport? And Cecilia?"

"Yeah, it's hard enough to picture now. Imagine if this had happened in high school."

"You'd have been scarred for life," Jack answered, his devilish grin returning. Then the music changed, and they found themselves at the center of the floor, hemmed in by the other dancers. All around them, couples drew close for the slow number.

Jack shifted, too, pulling Marcy into his arms. "Does it bother you?" he asked, his tone suddenly serious.

"What?" She almost jumped when his hands settled around her waist, warm and strong.

"Your mother and Mr. Rappaport?" He seemed perfectly at ease, completely unaware of the tension that stiffened her steps, unaware of the distraction his touch was causing her. Maybe it was Lizzy's wine, or the music, or . . . or nothing but her own silliness. After all, this was Jack, her best friend, the guy she'd known most of her life.

She realized Jack was studying her, looking concerned. "Mother and Mr. Rappaport," she repeated. "Why should it bother me? It might not come to anything, and if it does, at least I'll know she's happy. Plus, it'll give her something to keep her busy besides meddling in my life."

They danced in silence for a while, and she began to relax. "We've never done this before, have we?" Jack murmured. His voice, close to her ear, sent a delicious shiver down her spine. Not a chill, but intensely warm and exciting. The sensation unnerved her.

"Why not?" he added.

She swallowed back the lump forming in her throat. "Maybe because you always chose your partners for their bra size instead of their skill at tying a knot in fishing line."

A soft sigh whispered from his lips. "There are some things a guy just doesn't do with his best friend. Women come and go, but a guy's friend is different."

"Hey, I'm a woman—or haven't you noticed?" The flip comment slipped out more from habit than from any conscious thought.

"I've always noticed," he said. "You just never noticed me noticing."

"You never said anything."

"I wanted to, but I've always needed you more as a friend. I didn't want to risk losing that. Now I realize I was wrong."

*Friend.* He'd said friend, and that's what he was— her best friend. Reminding herself of that didn't ease the rapid beat of her heart, or the comfortable rightness in the feel of his hands about her waist. It didn't make her stop wanting to lean closer against him.

She told herself again it was the wine, that was all. But hidden memories emerged to refute that: The crush on him she'd developed, then put away, when she was fifteen and just starting to notice boys as something other than pests or fishing companions. Her sadness at watching him with one girl after another, then one woman after another. The fact she could tell him things she couldn't tell anyone—not even her mother. Not even her fiancé.

He knew her better than anyone, and she knew him the same way.

Her fingers shifted restlessly, and she noticed his pulse beating beneath her thumb in time with her own racing heart. She began to tremble. This was not how a woman was supposed to feel in the arms of her best friend.

# FOUR

The night took on a surreal tone. The music surrounded them, cooing and teasing in soft, mellow notes, inviting intimacy.

"Marcy?" Jack whispered, his breath warm at her ear. A shiver ran down her spine. The sensation tightened the fingers of confusion closing around Marcy's heart.

"Promise me something, Marcy," Jack continued.

"No pink taffeta for your tux. There's a place in town with a lovely lavender one, though. I was thinking it would look nice with an orchid boutonniere—or maybe sprigs of fresh lavender," she replied, striving for a light, bantering tone.

"Just so it's not pink roses," he answered. The rough, gravelly note in his voice caused her to pull away just enough to look him in the face. What she saw in his expression only fed her confusion.

Longing. For an instant, with the dim light from the bandstand in his face, she thought she glimpsed an unnamed wanting in the darkness of his eyes, in the solemn lines of his face. Roses, he'd said. The sweet, rich fragrance of them filled her senses, mingling with the scent of Jack, the woodsy cologne he wore, and the clean freshness beneath it. Jack.

Old, long-banished dreams fluttered gently to the surface of her memory, and her heart fluttered with them. *Why now?* she wondered. Was it simply that he always wished for what was out of reach—for what could be safely pined for but would never pin him down? Or was it simply her own nostalgia, combined with the potent mix of moonlight and his mother's wine?

"Why not roses?" she asked softly.

He grinned, the lines of his face curving into the characteristic, mocking smile she knew so well. "Pink roses—wild pink roses—always make me think of that spot down by the creek, you with your hair dangling down your back, your feet bare, and a smear of mud on your cheek while you reeled in a fat catfish and I waited with the net. And now here we are at the Rose Festival, dancing slow for the first time. I'd like to keep those memories in my mind, tied as they are to roses. I don't think I could stand it if I had to add the picture of you at the altar with Roger to the roses file. That just doesn't fit with the others."

It was a long speech for him, and far too serious to dismiss. "I know you don't like him, but—" she began, but he silenced her with a shake of his head.

"Let's just dance," he said, pulling her closer. She hesitated, wanting to say more, but lacking the conviction to argue. Her own thoughts and emotions were too muddled by the wine and the night.

Again she felt the soft, quick fluttering of her heartbeat, and an answering flutter in the pit of her stomach. The sensation felt familiar, yet oddly more

# THE BRIDE'S BEST MAN

intense than she could remember feeling before. Jack breathed a long sigh against her neck, then nuzzled her hair. She felt herself leaning into him, and she caught herself.

"Jack, what's happening here?" she asked softly.

A light, flirtatious laugh escaped him as he drew back and winked. "Honey, you've had some of Mother Lizzy's wine, judging from the fresh, fruity fragrance upon your breath. And I'm just being me," he answered, then whirled her around in a circle as the music shifted into a new song with a fast beat. "Did you forget I'm the devil's own, the spoiler of virtue, the guy every father in town warned his daughter about? And here you are, an engaged woman with no fiancé in sight to protect you. Fair game, I'd say."

"Can't help yourself, right?" Marcy wasn't fooled by his exaggerated leer or his teasing words. "Come on, I'm thirsty," she said as she slipped out of his embrace and tugged him along behind her.

A cooling breeze lifted the hair at the nape of her neck, but did nothing to ease the heat lingering within her. Nor did it chase away the doubts crowding her mind—doubts about Roger, about the wisdom of those moments in Jack's arms, about her own sense of direction. She'd been so sure she knew where she was going with her life, that she'd found a love worth keeping. Yet here she was at the mercy of the moon, the music, and her own traitorous emotions. She was supposed to be engaged, supposed to be planning marriage to the man of her dreams, the love of her life.

So why did a simple dance with Jack make her

heart race like a teenager's at the prom? Prewedding jitters? Or warning bells?

Marcy sighed, no longer sure of anything except that she should stay out of Lizzy's wine and Jack's arms. Neither was likely to contribute to clarity of thought, and that's what she needed right now.

Lizzy was waiting for them at the back of the booth with two cups already filled. "I thought you could use this after all that dancing."

"Water?"

"Would you rather have water?" Lizzy asked, her smile slipping. "Of course, I should have thought to ask. Silly me," she said, already heading toward a large cooler.

"Never mind, Mom, this is fine," Jack interjected. He took a sip of the wine and smiled his approval. "I just thought we'd check in and see if you wanted us to walk you back to the house."

"Oh, heavens no! How old do you think I am? I won't be ready to leave for hours. Now you two go on and leave us mature adults to our fun." She aimed a grin over her shoulder at her coworkers in the booth, both balding and thicker around the middle than they'd been at last year's festival. "Don't worry about me. The day I can't walk home alone I'll check myself into the nursing home and have them lock the door behind me."

"You tell 'em, Lizzy," one of the men interjected.

"Cramping your style, Mother?" Jack teased in a low voice, and Marcy was amused to see a blush spread up the older woman's neck to her cheeks.

"Learned a thing or two from you, Mr. Smartypants," she retorted with a light slap at his arm. "Now

# THE BRIDE'S BEST MAN

go mind your own business, both of you," she added, practically shoving them out the back door of the big booth.

"I guess she told us," Marcy said as they made their way through the crowd. "First my mother, now yours. Is it something in the water?"

"Must be the wine," Jack muttered. He emptied his cup in a long swallow, then crumpled it and dropped it into a trash can. Her own half-empty cup followed his with only a sliver of regret on her part for the waste. If it *was* the wine, she didn't need any more. And if it wasn't—well, she didn't want to consider that right now.

"Look, there's Mother and Mr. Rappaport," she said as she spotted the couple at a water fountain near the edge of the park. "Maybe it *is* the water."

Jack's answering laugh ended abruptly. He snatched up her hand, tugging with sudden urgency. "How about a walk down to the creek?"

She knew what creek he meant. Their creek. Their spot where the wild roses would be blooming, where the spent petals would be floating in the moonlight that reflected off the water's surface. "At this hour? Why?" Her voice trembled slightly, despite her attempt at nonchalance.

He stared over her head. "Because Penny Bartow is headed this way, and she has seduction written all over her." He started walking, pulling her along behind. "Don't argue. Just help me out, or I'll have to fight her off with a stick."

Marcy caught up with him and aimed a playful punch at his arm with her free hand. "Full of yourself, aren't you?"

He winced. "No, just sore. She's been pinching my backside all evening."

"You're making that up!" she accused.

"I could show you the marks." He tugged her behind an overgrown shrub near the corner.

"No, thanks, I—I—" she stammered and pulled away, feeling a flush of dangerous heat. He wasn't looking at her, though. She followed the direction of his gaze as he cautiously lifted a branch and peered down the street.

"Damn, she's coming this way!" he grumbled. "Let's go!"

"Why?" she demanded, resisting this time as he tried to pull her along behind him. "Why don't you just tell her you're not interested?"

"She thinks I'm playing hard to get."

"You? My goodness, what an imagination you have!"

His pained sigh held just enough real regret to dampen the teasing mood that had sprouted between them, leaving behind an awkward silence. "I guess I deserve that," he said after a moment. "Doesn't mean I won't make you pay for it, though," he added, sliding back behind the familiar, teasing mask.

And it was a mask, she realized. He used it to hide his real feelings, his real self, even from himself sometimes. She didn't have time to ponder the thought, though, because a second glance through the shrubbery revealed Penny's purposeful approach.

"Last one to the creek has to dig for the worms," she muttered as she slipped past him. He caught up with her easily, and took her hand as they maneuvered over the cracked, jutting sidewalk segments that had been displaced by the bulging roots of an ancient maple tree.

Excitement bubbled within her as they hurried past a streetlight and slipped into the shadows of an alley that ran behind the row of brick-faced business buildings opposite the park. They kept to the alley for three blocks, then emerged on a side street that wound down the hillside between rows of small, older houses.

"I think we've lost her," Marcy noted, slowing her pace as she sidestepped another large root protruding through a buckled section of sidewalk. Here, the streetlights were spaced farther apart, and the welcoming glow of porch lights left burning wasn't sufficient in most cases to safely illuminate the cracked sidewalks.

Once, Marcy had known the route so well she could have navigated it with her eyes closed, cracked sidewalks and all. But there were new cracks and buckles in the cement, and overgrown shrubs where she remembered only neatly trimmed rows.

Time had changed this street, had left its residents settling for less, willing to overlook greater flaws. Is that what had happened to her, too? With Roger was she settling for only half of what she wanted from life? The thought sent an unexpected shiver of unease down her spine.

"Someone walking on your grave?" Jack asked.

"Something like that." She wished he hadn't noticed, then was glad he had as he laid a comforting arm over her shoulders and tugged her against him.

"Don't worry, fair lady. I'll protect you from the

ghouls of the night, the scavengers who lurk in the dark, lying in wait for the pure and the innocent."

"And who will protect me from you?" she teased.

His steps faltered, and she glanced up, wishing the light weren't so dim here, wishing the nearly full moon had the strength to shine through the thickly leafed branches that shadowed his face. "Maybe I'm the one who needs protecting."

"From Penny?"

He shook his head, the movement barely discernable in the darkness. Shifting his weight from side to side, he dug his hands deep into his pockets. "From my own stupidity. All this time, I thought I knew what I wanted, where I was headed, and exactly what I was doing. Now it seems the future stretches ahead forever, and it's looking pretty lonely."

Backing up a step, he whistled tunelessly, then cocked his head to the side. She thought he was going to say something else, but he didn't. He turned abruptly and walked on, his steps stiff and slow until she caught up with him again.

She laid a hand on his arm, drawing his glance. An unexplained heat, much like that she'd experienced when they'd been dancing so close, traveled from her fingertips up her arm and all the way to the pit of her stomach. "It's not the end of our friendship. I promise you that," she said, her voice husky with emotion.

He nodded, looking unconvinced as they stepped into a gap in the trees left by the demise of an old honey locust tree whose stump sprouted thin, determined new growth at its base. The streetlight at the

# THE BRIDE'S BEST MAN

corner turned his face to harsh planes and shadows, accentuating the sadness in his expression.

Sliding her hand up his arm to touch his cheek, Marcy marveled at this man who was her friend, her best friend. "It won't change," she promised. "I won't let anything change."

He captured her hand in his own, his expression serious as he lifted her palm to his lips. "You can't stop it, sweetheart. It's changed already. Everything has." His husky tone betrayed a depth of emotion he rarely allowed voice. He kissed her palm again, as if for emphasis, and the burning intensity of his gaze reignited the confusion she'd felt while they were dancing.

And the heat. It simmered in his quiet stare, in the air between them, in the blood racing through her veins. She felt the burning deep within her, and her heartbeat quickened. But this was Jack, a small voice in the back of her mind insisted—Jack, her fishing buddy, the never serious man with the roaming eye and dry, sharp wit. Right now, his gaze wasn't roaming, and there was no sign of his characteristically wicked humor dancing in those dark eyes of his.

"Something has changed," she admitted, feeling unsure of herself and of this man who'd been her best friend for so long she couldn't remember a time when he hadn't been part of her life.

"I know. I wish—" He drew a deep breath. "Aw, what the hell," he whispered as he jerked her against him and kissed her hard.

Marcy froze with shock, but only for a second. Then the heat that had been building all evening within her, between the two of them, blossomed into something irresistible, something much sweeter than the fragrance of roses that filled the air around them. His fingers curled into the hair at the nape of her neck, holding her, caressing with gentle yet insistent pressure.

His tongue teased at her lips, asking, demanding. A boldness she didn't know she had overtook her senses. She tangled her fingers in his hair, opening her mouth to his, thrilling in the taste of him—mint and wine and something she couldn't quite define, something she knew was simply, irresistibly Jack.

A flicker of doubt teased her brain, but she shoved the thought away before it could take hold. She couldn't think now, wouldn't think. She needed to feel, to test this thing that had sprung up between them, to define it.

Her thumbs traced circles at his temples, and his fingers mirrored the movement against her shoulder blades.

Pleasure, that's what it was. Pure, unimaginable pleasure. For a moment, Marcy gave herself up to the sweet intensity of the kiss. No questions, no doubts, just him and her and this strange, sweet passion flaring between them.

Somewhere in the distance, a cat yowled. A door slammed, and a nearby porch light blinked off, then on again. Childish giggles intruded.

"Hey, rent a room!" a young voice called. More giggles followed, breaking the spell. Marcy froze, realizing where she stood, what she was doing. She dipped her head to rest her forehead against Jack's shoulder.

# THE BRIDE'S BEST MAN

Good heavens, she'd been making out on a street corner like an oversexed teenager. What could she have been thinking?

An older voice joined the children's, scolding and hurrying them along. Gradually, the laughter faded into the distance. Marcy couldn't move, though, couldn't grasp her way through her own confusion. Her hands trembled, and she realized she was clenching them together behind Jack's neck.

Jack's sigh filled the silence. Marcy felt his breath fanning her cheek, and she raised her face, fluttering her eyelids open. "That didn't happen. It couldn't have."

"It did," he said, eyeing her tenderly. A flicker of passion lingered in his gaze, as well, and it triggered a tremulous flutter deep within her.

No, this definitely wasn't how a woman was supposed to feel about her best friend. And this wasn't what an engaged woman should be doing with her best friend—or anyone else—in the absence of her fiancé.

The full import of what she'd just done, of the betrayal she'd just committed, hit her with the force of a physical blow. She unclenched her hands and backed away, tripping on the cracked sidewalk. Jack reached for her, but she caught herself without his help and spun around. She ran between the houses, losing herself in the darkness, ignoring his calls as she dived through a gap in the hedges. She hid in a shed for a few minutes until she was sure Jack had continued down the street.

She ran without regard for direction, for anything but the guilty images her mind kept replaying. Jack's touch. Jack's kiss. Him and her, tangled together beneath the streetlight.

And when she realized she couldn't outrun them, she sank onto the ground, feeling the dampness of dew on her knees and the sharp poke of a stone against her tender flesh. She shifted, and the moonlight caught the sparkle of the diamond in her engagement ring. A pained sob caught in her throat as she touched the stone, thinking of all it signified.

Wine and moonlight. She'd never imagined the combination could be so potent, or that it could engender such a betrayal of good sense. She slid lower, rolling onto her back to stare up at the moon. She shouldn't have come back here without Roger, shouldn't have touched the wine, shouldn't have fallen prey to Jack's practiced charm.

After all these years, she'd thought herself immune to him. She didn't blame him. One didn't blame the wind for blowing or a cat for climbing a tree. He'd simply done what was in his nature. And she, fool that she was, had simply lost her mind. There could be no other explanation, not for someone who knew Jack as well as she did.

Jack slapped his palm angrily against the stucco wall in the alley across from the festival. His mind barely registered the sting of the bumpy surface against his flesh. It was nothing compared to the pain swelling in his chest. He flushed hot, then cold, as he remembered the look on Marcy's face as she'd backed away from him.

Shock. Guilt. A trace of longing mingled with hurt. And betrayal.

He had to be the biggest idiot on the face of the earth. All these years he'd known her, and he hadn't realized how much she truly meant to him. And when he finally figured it out, he'd bungled things badly. A man with his experience, with his reputation, should be able to tell a woman how he felt and leave her feeling good about it. Instead, he'd only managed to confuse and complicate her life and hurt her badly in the bargain. He knew that because he knew her. Right now, she had to be feeling lower than a bottom-feeding catfish.

But that was just it. He had no experience when it came to confessing love. He'd never done it before—had never even wanted to, not to please a woman, not to manipulate one into his arms. A wry smirk twisted his lips. Even a scoundrel had to have some standards.

Besides, he wasn't really sure it *was* love—at least not the kind of love Marcy wanted. He wasn't sure he was capable of being the kind of man she needed. All he knew was Roger wasn't going to make her happy, and Jack could. Maybe.

Aw, hell, he stood a better chance of making her happy than stiff-upper-lip Roger with the fancy car and house, a man who hadn't a clue how the sunlight reflected off the surface of a still lake could light a golden glow on Marcy's cheeks. Or how she looked with the thrill of a catch sparkling in her eyes even for a mere six-inch bluegill—because, as she always insisted, the fish were biting, and the big guys sent the little ones on ahead to see what was happening.

*What's really going on here?* Marcy had asked as they danced. He still didn't know. He should have just told her what he was thinking, that she was still the most beautiful, most interesting woman he'd ever met, that she was too good for a stuffed shirt like Roger Ashforth. *Don't marry the jerk,* he should have said. *He's not right for you.*

Damn it, he *had* told her that, and she'd insisted she knew what she was doing. Well, she didn't, and tonight Jack had proved it. No woman in love with another man could have kissed Jack the way Marcy had. If she loved Roger as much as she said she did, she wouldn't have trembled in his arms, wouldn't have reacted with such passion.

"Idiot," he repeated, barely a whisper this time. What good was it to be right? He stood alone in an alley, feeling lower than dirty gum under a rock, and Marcy was out there somewhere alone, hurting and angry.

He had to find her. He'd run out of places to look, though. She wasn't at the creek or at home, and no one he'd spoken to along the way to either place had seen her. Either she didn't want to be found—at least by him—or she'd gone back to the festival.

He froze, then slapped his hand against the wall again. Of course. He should have guessed. That's exactly what she must have done—an act so typically Marcy he couldn't believe he hadn't thought of it immediately.

She'd push the kiss out of her mind as quickly as she could, pretend it had never happened. What better way to do that than in a crowd of people who'd known her all her life? She'd barely have time to get a word in edgewise among the small-town gossip and chatter. She'd use that to crowd out any disturbing thoughts, any doubts that kiss might have engendered.

That bothered him almost as much as the idea of her sitting alone somewhere, heartbroken, confused, and crying.

He took off toward the lights of the festival, his long stride determined and swift. No way would he let her forget that kiss. No way would he let her shove him out of her mind so easily.

Jack found Cecilia standing at the edge of the dance floor with Mr. Rappaport. The older man winked as he approached, and held his paper cup aloft in a mock salute. "Nice night, eh? Can't remember when we've had better weather for the festival."

Jack nodded his agreement. "I suppose," he answered vaguely, his concern elsewhere. "Have either of you seen Marcy?"

"Last I saw her she was dancing with you," Cecilia answered.

Rappaport's eyebrows arched with amusement. "I spotted the two of you sneaking off through the trees a while back. Gave you the slip, did she?"

Jack felt a heated flush creep up his neck. He couldn't remember the last time he'd blushed with embarrassment. Or shame. "Something like that," he murmured. "We had a—um—" he fumbled for an explanation. "We disagreed about something. I need to explain."

Cecilia looked unconcerned. "She's just touchy, what with the wedding and all."

Jack wished it were that simple. "Maybe," he answered, not wanting to confess the truth. Cecilia was slow to anger, but when riled, her tongue was as sharp as his own mother's. And Jack's actions tonight would most certainly raise Cecilia's ire.

"We'll point her your way if we see her," Ed said, his expression mild. A hint of suspicion colored his gaze when he met Jack's eyes, and Jack felt his flush deepen.

"I'd appreciate that," Jack muttered, hurrying away. He scanned the crowd, searching for a glimpse of Marcy's dark, silky hair, as he headed for the refreshment stand where Lizzy still was dispensing soft drinks, beer, and chips and holding court with her two balding coworkers.

"What did you do to the poor girl?" Lizzy demanded after hearing Jack had lost track of Marcy.

"What makes you think I did anything to her?" Jack countered.

His mother simply arched her brows and glared in the time-honored fashion of all mothers who know their offspring have committed some infraction. Guilt pricked his conscience, but he'd long ago learned confessing to Lizzy didn't accomplish anything useful. It just made the frown lines at the corner of her mouth deepen with disappointment and brought on the type of scolding he'd prefer to avoid right now.

"Just let me know if you see her," he said after a moment.

"And where will you be?"

He grimaced. "Looking for her."

"Oh, well, that's helpful," she retorted.

"Please tell her I'm looking for her," he corrected, then hesitated before adding, "and tell her I'm sorry."

Lizzy's brows knit together in a frown of concern. "What did you do?" she demanded quietly, stepping closer.

"Nothing," he retorted automatically, then paused at the disbelief in her expression. "Everything. I screwed up, really screwed up this time. I can be such an idiot sometimes—but you already knew that, didn't you?"

Her frown softened as she placed a hand against his cheek. "Foolish, maybe. A little blind sometimes. You'll make things right. You always do," she said. "And Marcy knows you well enough to forgive whatever you said."

Jack wasn't so sure. "I hope so," he told Lizzy. "I'm not so sure."

Lizzy didn't answer, and he realized he'd been hoping she'd reassure him. It was expecting too much. Lizzy had never been one for false promises or false hopes. "Just do your best, and whatever happens is what happens," she said after a moment.

He nodded slowly and made his escape.

He searched the park grounds twice, called Cecilia's house from a pay phone, then searched the park again without a sign of her. A check of the house revealed her car was still in the driveway, although the house was firmly locked and there were no lights on.

She wasn't hiding inside, he decided. She wouldn't. By now, she'd have built up a healthy head of steam and would be itching to release it in his direction. She'd have stormed out the door in answer to his knock if she'd been there.

Disconsolate, he wandered back toward the lights and music, which had once again slowed into a mellow, nostalgic ballad. He was almost to the bandstand when he spotted her strolling along the sidewalk that connected the fountain at the center of the town square with the semicircle of benches by the bandstand.

She looked sad and thoughtful and so beautiful he thought his chest would burst with the tangle of emotions just the sight of her evoked. He shifted directions and intercepted her before she could join the throng.

"Marcy?" He touched her arm, drawing her attention as he stepped up beside her.

She froze, then dropped her gaze to the sidewalk. "I really don't want to talk to you right now," she said. The words, though softly spoken, caught like a giant fishhook that pierced the flesh with its barbed tip, then refused to pull free.

"And I really don't want to pretend nothing happened," Jack replied.

Her chin tilted upward, and she cautiously met his gaze. He saw uncertainty in her eyes, and just a hint of something more, something that made his heartbeat falter, then resume at an increased pace.

"I couldn't do that," she admitted. "It happened. I'm just not sure what to do about it."

He caught her hand in his own and felt her stiffen with resistance. "Let's walk," he suggested. "Let's just walk and talk, or maybe find a bench somewhere so we can sit down and sort through this."

"I don't think I can do that right now."

He nodded slowly, understanding, yet reluctant to leave so much unsaid.

"I really need to sort this out," he said, trying not to sound as desperate as he felt. He couldn't let this night end badly. If he did, he'd lose her, and not just as the lover he'd only recently begun to imagine. He'd lose her friendship, too. The thought was unbearable.

Tentatively, she closed her fingers around his and let him lead her through the park. They found an unoccupied bench in a far corner beneath an ancient spreading maple.

They sat in silence for a moment before Jack gathered the courage to voice his thoughts. "I tried to follow you," he said at last. "You always could run faster than me, although how you did it in those blasted sandals, I don't know. I must be getting old."

A shaky laugh escaped her. "I hid in the Murdocks' shed until you passed," she admitted. "Then I wound up in Tallgrass Field."

An expletive escaped him. "I didn't think of looking there." They'd played there sometimes as children, though not much since the city fathers had frowned on people tramping through what then were new wildflower and prairie grass plantings.

"You wouldn't have found me anyway."

Because she didn't want to be found, he finished in his head. Because he'd overstepped the bounds of friendship—way overstepped. "I'm sorry," he murmured. As the words passed through his lips, he recognized them as a lie. "No, I'm not sorry. I know I should be, and I didn't set out to do it. It wasn't planned. That kiss was more instinct than conscious thought."

"Just couldn't help yourself, right? I mean, it was either me or Penny, since we're probably the only unattached females between twenty-six and sixty in town tonight, and you figured I wouldn't pinch."

He met her glare head-on. "You kissed me back."

"It was the wine," she retorted, looking away.

He considered that for a moment. "Maybe. You used to hold your liquor a lot better than that, though."

"And you didn't," she snapped back. "Maybe that's all it was. Why else would you suddenly kiss me after all these years?" Pain shimmered in her gaze before she turned her face pointedly away, hiding whatever else he might have read in her expression.

He leaned forward, resting his face in his hands while he considered how to answer. He wasn't sure he understood it himself, not completely. He straightened, raking a hand through his hair as he swallowed back a lump of uncertainty. He'd always hidden his feelings behind a wall of humor, poked fun at what was too serious to dwell on for long. But that, he realized, was cheating. Marcy deserved better. She deserved an honest answer—or at least an answer as honest as he could make it at the moment.

"Maybe because I didn't think I had much left to lose," he admitted.

Irritated, she shifted, turning so she could see his face in the filtered moonlight. "I thought we already covered that."

"As I recall, that was the prelude to the kiss."

Her lips tightened into a frown, and he could see

in her expression she remembered it that way, too. And it disturbed her.

"It wasn't just the wine, Marcy," he insisted.

She squeezed her eyes closed and a single tear trailed down her cheek. "I know."

# FIVE

Marcy thought it appropriate that she awoke early Sunday morning to the crash of thunder. Outside, the wind slashed through the trees. A branch tapped an irregular beat against the roof. Then the rain struck with startling force, splattering huge drops against the window beside her bed.

She snuggled deeper beneath the thick comforter, wishing for the sweet oblivion of deep, dreamless sleep. All night she'd tossed and turned, dozing fitfully, disturbed by restless dreams she couldn't remember. All that remained of them was a vague sense of unease. And why not? She'd done the unthinkable, the impossible.

She'd kissed her best friend. She'd kissed Jack. Really kissed him, with heartthrobbing, toe-curling passion. She'd lost track of time and place, something that had never happened with Roger. Nor could she remember feeling so cherished, so warmed with sweet intensity.

Kissing Roger was . . . pleasant. But he'd never made her toes curl, and he'd never made her forget where she was. She wasn't sure what to think about this strange development or what she wanted to do about it—what she ought to do about it. Her only certainty was that she wasn't ready to marry Roger, not when another man could affect her so deeply.

A soft knock at the door startled her. "Jack?" she whispered.

The door swung open to reveal Cecilia, her expression indignant as she bustled into the room, her heavy cotton gown billowing around her. "I should think not. The two of you aren't children anymore. You stopped that sneaking back and forth nonsense years ago—didn't you?"

"Of course." Marcy raked her tousled hair back from her face. "I was just dreaming about—oh, never mind," she finished, abandoning the lie before it was half formed.

Cecilia yawned and blinked owlishly at her daughter before glancing around the room. Marcy thought for an instant Cecilia was looking for Jack anyway, that she'd check under the bed and in the closet. Her mother simply glanced at one window, then stepped around the bed and closed the other.

A brief memory of one of last night's dreams flashed through her mind: Jack climbing through the window and kissing her senseless, and Roger climbing out from under the bed and demanding they stop.

Marcy shook her head, attempting to chase away the weird thought. "What time is it?"

Cecilia shrugged. "Six or so. Go back to sleep. I didn't mean to wake you. I just wanted to make sure the windows were closed in here. I polished the floor Friday, and I don't want to have to deal with spots."

Marcy nodded, then hesitated. "Why did you knock?"

Cecilia yawned and blinked owlishly. "Habit, I suppose. Sweet dreams, dear." She backed out and shut the door softly behind her, leaving Marcy staring suspiciously at the closed door.

*Habit?* Marcy's mother could be odd at times, but she wasn't that odd. Maybe she suspected something was up with the two of them. Maybe she half expected to find Jack here. And maybe she'd just been channeling into Marcy's restless dreams. The image of the Jack and Roger dream returned, drawing a low groan from Marcy as she slid beneath the covers and pulled a pillow over her head.

An hour later, she gave up trying to sleep. Or read. Or watch television. "What time is it in London?" she muttered. Six hours before or six hours after. Not that it mattered. She couldn't exactly cancel the wedding via a transoceanic telephone call, even if she did manage to track Roger down, which she probably wouldn't be able to do.

Maybe he'd call her.

And then what would she say? "Hey, Roger! We can't get married 'cause I dreamed all night about sleeping with Mr. Maid of Honor. Oh, and by the way, I really did kiss him last night."

Nope. She couldn't do it, not that way.

She dragged herself out of bed and shuffled to the window. The storm had faded into a light rain. In the distance, she could see a patch of sunshine through a gap in the clouds. It was going to be another steamy summer day in Bridgeton.

A movement at the corner of her vision caught her

attention, and she swung her gaze toward the house next door. Jack stood at the window opposite her, his shirt unbuttoned, his hair damp from the shower. A cautious smile touched his lips. She stood there, feeling the heat of his stare like a physical touch.

On impulse, she unlatched the window and pushed it open. "Hey you!" she called as he opened his own.

"Nice nightie," he answered and winked broadly.

Marcy glanced down at her faded Loony Tunes sleep shirt and grinned. "A friend gave it to me," she answered. Four years ago—no, five—he'd wrapped it in pink and purple printed fish paper and hidden a box of hand-tied trout flies in the folds. Then he'd let her think he'd forgotten her birthday. She'd found the package in the refrigerator after he'd gone home.

"Yeah, I remember."

"Is that Marcy?" Lizzy's voice carried through the open windows from somewhere in the house as clearly as a loon call over a lake.

"Good morning, Lizzy," Marcy called out. "Did you have a good time last night?"

"Apparently," Jack interjected. "She dragged in after one, whistling and singing off-tune. Woke up half the neighborhood cats."

"I wasn't whistling. That was Mr. Rappaport. He and Bob Jackson walked us home," Lizzy answered with a good-natured tweak to Jack's ear. "Morning, dear," the woman added. "Coming to church?" Lizzy wore a patterned blue dress Marcy hadn't seen before and a dozen or so hot rollers stuck haphazardly around the top of her head.

"I'm not sure. I'm still waking up," Marcy answered.

"I could stay home to keep you company," Jack offered, a devilish glint dancing in his dark eyes.

"Absolutely not," Lizzy interjected. "You're going to the education committee meeting with me, and then you're going to sit with me through the morning service. It's one thing to dance with a man on Saturday night, but if he thinks I'm going to leave a space open in the pew next to me on Sunday morning in front of God, Reverend Baxter, and everyone, then he has another think coming." A high flush had colored her features by the time she finished. She tapped her son's chest with a pointed, pink-polished fingernail for emphasis with every third word. "So get a move on it, buster," she finished, then stalked off.

Marcy gaped in confusion. "What did I miss?"

"Apparently Bob Jackson's intentions are honorable."

"And your mother's aren't," Marcy surmised.

A trace of his sinfully wicked grin remained. "That about sizes up the situation."

His amusement ignited an answering smile. "This could be interesting," she mused. "I think I'll see you at church." The idea seemed more appealing than moping alone here at the house, stewing on her own suddenly tangled relationships. She'd already decided what she had to do. All that remained was the opportunity, and that wouldn't come until Roger returned from London. In the meantime, she could use the distraction.

Her mother had fresh coffee and rolls waiting in

the kitchen. She glanced up from the newspaper when Marcy entered and smiled. The faint blue shadows beneath her eyes were the only sign she'd been up past two a.m. Otherwise, she was her usual perky, energetic self. Marcy lifted the coffeepot and fumbled for a mug.

"I heard you talking to Jack and Lizzy. They're going in early?"

"Lizzy has a committee meeting." Marcy stirred a thick dollop of cream into her coffee and took a grateful sip. She loved Cecilia's coffee. It was her mother's one indulgence. She bought the beans from a specialty shop in the city, ground them fresh for each pot, and always drank it with thick, rich cream provided by a local farmer's prize Jersey cows.

"You look tired, dear," Cecilia murmured. "Do you want to stay home and rest this morning?"

Marcy shook her head, her mind already made up on that point. "I'll just get to bed early tonight. We're leaving at the usual time?"

Her mother nodded as she pushed the basket of rolls toward Marcy and handed her a small, cut-glass plate. "Have you given any further thought to having the wedding here in town? I know the Ashforths have other ideas, but it really is the bride's choice, and it would be so lovely to have the ceremony in our own church now that the windows have all been restored and the pews refinished. I just think—"

"Mom, please, " Marcy interrupted. "Let's just forget about the wedding for now."

"Forget it? You haven't decided on the flowers yet or the invitations or even on a date. You'd think you didn't really want to get married."

Marcy stared down at her plate, unsure how much to tell her mother, unsure whether it was wise to tell her anything at all at this point.

"Marcy?"

She took a bite of a sweet roll, stalling.

Cecilia touched her arm. "You *do* want to get married, don't you?"

The cloying sweetness of the cinnamon roll couldn't negate the bitter discomfort that griped Marcy. She chewed, swallowed, and washed it down with a gulp of coffee. "I kissed Jack last night," she blurted out, then took another gulp of coffee.

"Jack?" Shock held Cecilia still for a moment. Then her fingers fluttered in the air. "Oh, darn, I was afraid of something like that. When the two of you ran off, and then he couldn't find you, and—oh, Marcy, what were you thinking?"

A rueful laugh burst from her. "Apparently I wasn't thinking at all," Marcy said.

"Oh, dear, what a mess."

Marcy thought that might be the understatement of the year. Feeling slightly queasy, she pushed her plate away and leaned on her elbows. Chin on her palm, she studied her mother's concerned expression. "Sorry, Mother. I know this throws a kink in your plans."

"*My* plans! What are *you* going to do? You're not going to tell Roger, are you?"

"How can I not tell him?" Marcy released a heavy sigh. "Not that I want to, but I can't see I have a choice."

"Of course you have a choice," Cecilia retorted.

"You don't think I told your father everything, do you?"

"Did you ever kiss another man?"

"Of course. Did you think I married the first man who asked me?"

"After you were engaged."

Cecilia flushed, then stood. She chewed at her lip, then spun around and retrieved the coffeepot from the counter.

Her eyebrows arching with suspicion, Marcy followed her mother's nervous movements. "Mother? You didn't. Did you?"

Cecilia heaved an exasperated sigh. "Well, if you must know, I was engaged when I met your father. I broke off with Ed that night, and your father and I eloped a week later."

Marcy gaped. Never in a hundred years would she have guessed that straitlaced, proper Cecilia Winters would have committed such an impetuous act. "And you never thought to fill me in on this bit of family trivia?"

Cecilia huffed. "You didn't need to know. I was afraid you'd get some romantic notion in your head and run off and do the same. Had I known how long you'd drag your feet about this wedding, I would have told you sooner. Maybe that would have lighted a fire under you, and you'd be married already and not fall into such foolishness. Really, kissing Jack? I know he's Lizzy's boy, and he was never really a bad boy just— well, you know. He could get you into such trouble! Some of those scrapes nearly had me pulling my hair out. And it doesn't appear he's grown up much in that respect."

"As I recall, we got each other in trouble," Marcy replied.

"Hmmph." Cecilia picked up her mug, then thunked it back down, sloshing coffee over the edge. She didn't even seem to notice the mess, which in itself was a sign of her agitation. "Just don't do anything foolish. No, never mind that. Just don't make it worse."

"That's what I've been thinking about, not making it worse. That's why I'm calling off the wedding."

"Marcy, no!" Cecilia's hand fluttered near her throat. Then she crossed her arms, as if against a chill.

"I can't very well marry Roger under the circumstances. It wouldn't be right. You of all people should understand that. What if you'd married that other guy, feeling as you did about Dad?"

"I was in love with your father."

"Not what's-his-name."

"Ed." Cecilia's lined face radiated worry, and more than a little indignation.

"Ed," Marcy repeated, staring thoughtfully at her mother. "Ed who?"

"We're talking about you."

"Not Mr. Rappaport!"

Cecilia's indignant flush deepened. "We grew up in the same neighborhood. We were young, and we didn't know anything about life. Heavens, I really thought I was in love with him until I met your father and figured out what was what."

"And he's been carrying a torch for you ever since."

An unladylike snort burst from Cecilia. "Hardly.

The man's had two wives and six children. I've known him for ages—since grade school, at least. Kind of like you and Jack, except, well, Ed wasn't such a rascal. And your father was—well, so interesting. He'd been so many places, done so many things. Kind of like Roger."

Marcy blinked, the parallels eluding her. She wasn't sure what point her mother was trying to make, except that she didn't want Marcy to break the engagement. The rest wasn't making a lot of sense.

"Oh, goodness, look at the time. We'd better hurry if we're going to make it to the morning services." Cecilia flicked the coffeepot switch to the off position. "Maybe you should stay here, see if you can call Roger in London. You're just missing him."

"You think I kissed Jack because I was lonely?"

"What else could it be? You're certainly not in love with him—not that it would do you any good if you were. He's no more likely to marry than Lizzy, and we both know pigs will fly before that happens."

Marcy sighed. "Marriage isn't the ultimate goal here."

"Then what is?" Concern softened Cecilia's expression, stalling the biting retort that hung on the tip of Marcy's tongue. "I just want you to be happy, dear. That's all a mother wants for her child," Cecilia continued. "It's all I truly want for you. The rest is just frills, something to brag about at the weekly bingo tournament." She finished with a dismissive wave of her hand and busied herself tidying up the counter and rinsing the crumbs from the plates.

Relief threaded itself among the confused emotions tugging at Marcy's heart. Of all the reactions she'd anticipated from her mother, this wasn't one of them. "Thanks for understanding, Mother," she said, her voice almost a whisper as she gave Cecilia a quick hug.

"Just don't do anything impulsive. Don't break off the engagement just yet," Cecilia urged. "Be sure of yourself."

"That's backward, Mother. I should be sure of myself to stay engaged, not to break it off." She set her dishes in the sink and made her escape before the tears pricking at her eyelids could spill onto her cheeks.

To Marcy's relief, Cecilia didn't bring up the subject of the wedding or the about-to-be-broken engagement as they readied themselves or during the drive across town to the quaint brick church with its tall, glistening stained glass windows and old-fashioned bell tower. The bells were ringing as they drove into the parking lot, drawing a hiss of irritation from Cecilia. "Lizzy's going to have my hide for not being early," she muttered. "Just drop me at the steps."

At least, Marcy thought as she watched her mother slam the door and hurry up the steps, her mother's attention had switched to someone else's love life. She appreciated the respite, however brief it might prove to be.

Two friends from her high school days cornered her in the parking lot, so it was almost time for the service to begin when she finally made her way inside. Cecilia's anxious wave caught her attention and she slid into the pew next to her mother near the front of the church where she'd spent hundreds of other Sunday mornings.

"Move over here by me," Lizzy said, patting the empty bench beside her. "We can catch up." Her gaze, however, slid past Marcy with a triumphant tilt of her chin. Marcy didn't need to turn around to guess who that unspoken message was intended for.

"Thank you, my dear. You just saved my life, and certainly my social life," Lizzy whispered while she made a show of studying the church bulletin. "I can't imagine where Jack's at. He was supposed to guard my left."

"Always glad to help," Marcy muttered. A moment later, Jack appeared at the end of the pew, a sheepish expression on his face as he met his mother's glare. Instead of sliding into the empty spot by Cecilia, he edged along the row until he was next to Marcy. He unbuttoned his jacket and eased onto the seat, wincing.

"Hasn't gotten any softer through the years," he muttered, then leaned against Marcy as he reached past her to touch his mother's arm. "Sorry I'm late. Penny Bartow and her mother cornered me in the upper hallway, and it took me a while to get away."

"I'll bet," Lizzy retorted, sounding as if she didn't believe he'd even tried.

Her pique didn't seem to bother him. He smiled at Marcy, his lips twitching at the corners. She knew he was thinking of last night, of their flight through shadowed alleys, and that she wished she hadn't been so helpful. Then his gaze shifted lower, settling on the slit in her skirt, which had fallen open when she crossed her legs.

Slashing him a glare, she covered her leg. "We're in church," she whispered.

"I'd noticed. Did you talk to Roger this morning?"

"I left a message at his hotel—not that it's any of your business."

"Just wanting to know whether I need to brush up on my boxing skills before I go back to the city."

"What boxing skills?"

"Exactly." He leaned closer, his breath fanning her ear. "You're not wearing the rock."

"Your point?"

"Where's the engagement ring?" he asked bluntly.

"I don't want to talk about this now," she answered, keeping her voice low. "Especially not now and especially not here." She'd come here for distraction, for the sense of peace she'd often found in this place.

Two elderly ladies slid into the other end of the booth, followed by Mr. Rappaport and Bob Johnson, who cast a longing stare in Lizzy's direction. Jack made a show of shifting closer to Marcy to make room for the others in the pew, much to the amusement of Mr. Rappaport. Marcy heard Cecilia's irritated sigh and shot her mother a warning glance.

"I didn't say a word," Cecilia snapped.

"About what?" Lizzy asked.

"Nothing. Mother and I had a little disagreement this morning. That's all," Marcy explained.

"About what?" Jack asked.

Exasperated, Marcy pinched his leg just like she had when they were fifteen and he'd embarrassed her in front of the captain of the football team. "None of your business," she snapped.

He winced, rubbing the spot. "What is it about the women in this town?"

# THE BRIDE'S BEST MAN

"Oh, get over yourself," Marcy said.

"Jack, did you do something to make Roger angry?" Lizzy asked.

Cecilia snorted. "I'd say so."

"Mother!" Marcy's exclamation fell into a brief silence, so it seemed louder than she'd intended. She glanced around, noting several interested stares from the neighboring pews. "Drop it, please."

"Drop what?" Lizzy asked, her eyes alight with curiosity. "Jack, I told you this bridesmaid thing was a bad idea, bound to cause all sorts of problems."

"Actually, I'm the maid of honor," Jack corrected. "Or I was."

"Shh, the choir's coming in," Marcy hissed.

"Will somebody please tell me what's going on?" Lizzy insisted. "Marcy, did you fire him as the maid of honor?"

"He kissed her," Cecilia said. "Can you believe it? Jack kissed Marcy."

A low groan rose from Marcy's throat. She closed her eyes and shrank back against the pew, wishing she could sink beneath the polished floorboards and disappear. A light tap on her knee drew her attention, and she opened her eyes to find the elderly woman next to Jack staring at both of them. Mrs. Anderson had recently moved to town to live with her son and daughter-in-law, according to the recitation Cecilia had delivered yesterday morning on the walk in to the festival.

"It's probably none of my business, dear, but I thought you were engaged to a nice young rich man named Roy," Mrs. Anderson said.

"Roger," Jack corrected. "I'm hoping she'll dump him."

"That's it, I'm leaving," Marcy muttered. She stood with jerky movements, bumping against Lizzy in her hurry to get away from Jack, from all of them. She scooted past the others in the row and practically ran for the double doors. Once outside, she leaned against the cool bricks and closed her eyes.

Never in her entire life had she felt so embarrassed, so humiliated. Slow torture was too good for Jack Rathert. It probably was too good for her mother, too.

"Jeeminy Christmas, the woman has a big mouth," she muttered. She started toward the car, then realized she'd left her purse inside the church, and with it the keys. "Great, just great." No way would she go back inside after it.

She stomped down the steps and started across the parking lot. Behind her, she heard the door open, then Jack's call. She refused to acknowledge his presence.

He caught up with her halfway to the street and took her arm. She shook herself free and kept walking.

"You forgot your purse."

"So?"

"I brought it."

"Keep it," she snapped.

"OK," he answered, his tone noncommittal. "I like the color. Real leather, too, though a little sleek for your usual style. Did Roger pick this out?"

She ignored him and just kept walking. At the corner, she turned left, heading toward Main Street.

# THE BRIDE'S BEST MAN

"Got any candy in here? Or any change? There's a vending machine at the gas station up the street."

She heard the rasp of the zipper and halted, glaring at him. He'd dug into the side pocket and was pulling out a cloth case containing feminine personal products. "What's this?"

"Give me that, you idiot." She snatched it from him, then grabbed her purse and tucked the case back into place.

"Sorry," he answered with a shrug. "I missed breakfast."

"You did not."

"OK, I didn't. I'm still hungry, although I suppose a cozy cup of coffee at the Main Street diner is out of the question."

"How perceptive."

"At least you're speaking to me now."

She swung the purse at him, whacking him across the chest. "I ought to hang you by your toenails from the nearest tree. Why couldn't you keep your mouth shut?"

"I didn't—"

She swung the purse at him again, but this time he caught it. His strong, callused hands curled around the soft leather, then tightened as she tried to pull it out of his grasp. "Give me that!"

"Are you gonna hit me again?"

"I should."

His brows arched, and he gave her that slow, sheepish smile. He knew exactly how disarming it was, and she fought the weakening within her.

"You can just wipe that puppy dog look off your face. I don't like being manipulated."

He looked contrite. "You're right. I was out of line. We all were. I shouldn't have asked about the ring. It's really none of my business."

"Exactly."

He stroked a fingertip along the length of her cheek. "That kiss—it let something loose inside my head. Maybe it was a mistake. It didn't feel like a mistake, but if you think it was, I'll do my best to forget about it and go back to the way things were before."

Honesty shimmered in his warm, brown eyes. She drew a deep breath, knowing she could give him nothing less than the truth herself.

"It wasn't a mistake," she whispered.

# SIX

Days later, Marcy could still feel the glow that had radiated from Jack's eyes at her words.

"It wasn't a mistake," she'd repeated as she splayed a hand across his chest, stalling him as he reached for her. "But it's one heck of a complication."

"Meaning?" He'd folded her hand in his and raised it to his lips. The tremor in his fingertips puzzled her, and she'd studied his expression through narrowed eyes.

"You're not that dense," she'd whispered.

"Sshh, you'll ruin my reputation," he'd whispered back. Understanding softened his expression, and she'd felt the tension ease from her shoulders.

None of her confusion had faded, but she didn't have to sort out her thoughts and emotions all at once. She'd take it one step at a time. First, she had to let Roger know she'd had a change of heart. Then she could try to figure out exactly what that change meant.

Jack had walked her back to her mother's house. They talked of mundane things because she didn't want to talk about the mess she'd made of her life. She left a note for her mother, then headed back to the city alone. She needed time to think, to figure out how to tell Roger—and how much to tell him.

She couldn't get him on the phone. After three days of international phone tag, she was ready to stomp in a circle and scream with frustration.

A knock at her office door startled her into the present. "Yes?" she called out.

"Phone call while you were in the meeting," replied a young woman with owlish glasses and an impossibly short skirt. "Sorry I didn't get this to you sooner, but it got shuffled to the bottom of the pile by accident. I just found it."

"Roger?"

The secretary nodded. "Sorry." Marcy stared down at the pink message sheet and groaned.

*If it's about the wedding, talk to my mother. See you soon.*

*Roger*

This wasn't exactly the kind of news one delivered through the mother of the groom. Marcy wasn't sure there was a right way or a good way to deliver this kind of message, just that that wasn't it.

"Anything else?" she asked the secretary, disappointed there hadn't been a message from Jack, too.

"Just a couple of questions on the Reynolds account, but I pulled the numbers they needed from the files. No big deal. I'm heading out. See you tomorrow."

"Thanks," Marcy said, turning away to hide her disappointment. She and Jack had agreed she'd call

# THE BRIDE'S BEST MAN

him after she'd settled things with Roger, and she hadn't been able to do that yet.

Still, she missed the sound of his voice. Until this week, she hadn't realized how frequently they talked, how much she counted on his wry humor to break through the tension of her day.

Outside, the setting sun slanted golden light through the atrium windows down the hall from Marcy's office. She released an irritated sigh at the sight—or, rather, at the waste of another perfectly beautiful day spent sitting inside at a desk, shuffling paperwork and waiting for the phone to ring.

Well, it had rung—all day, almost nonstop, yet she still hadn't been able to talk to either of the people she really needed to speak with. Roger had called when she was in a conference room with a client. Jack hadn't called at all.

Maybe she'd call him tonight.

The thought lightened her mood immediately. She glanced at the clock. Almost eight, late enough that she didn't have to face so many hours alone in the apartment surfing channels and jumping with mixed relief and dread at every ring of the telephone.

After quick stops at the grocery store and an overnight dry cleaner's, she headed for her apartment, feeling the first whisper of anticipation she'd experienced in days. The sound of her phone ringing through her locked apartment door when she arrived home turned the whisper into a shout. *Jack*, she thought. She hoped.

Balancing a grocery bag on her hip, she slipped her key into the lock. She fumbled with the door, which was sticking again, then swung her hip against it hard, almost upsetting the groceries.

Juggling the slipping bag, her purse, and the suede briefcase Roger had given her for Christmas, she hurried inside just in time to hear the answering machine pick up. By the time she'd stowed the groceries on the hall table and the rest of her things on the floor beside it, her mother launched into one of her long, rambling messages.

Marcy leaned back against the wall, rubbing at the back of her neck as disappointment seeped through her. Again. She ought to pick up the phone, but she couldn't summon the patience to deal with Cecilia right now, not with her repeated apologies, well meant as they were, nor with the new list of suggestions for graciously handling the many details of canceling the wedding.

"I'm taking a shower," she muttered, her good mood having evaporated. Before she reached the bathroom, the phone rang again. This time it was Roger.

She snatched up the receiver, cutting off the message he'd begun. "Roger! I've been trying to reach you for days," she exclaimed.

"I know. I'm at the airport now. I'm on my way to my parents' house. They're having dinner with some investors, and Father wants me there in case they have any questions about the project. Did you talk to Mother?"

"No, Roger. This is something you and I need to discuss."

"I'm sure whatever you decide will be fine. The wedding details are more the bride's department anyway. The only thing we have to agree on is a date. Frankly, you'd be better off discussing that with my secretary. She knows my schedule better than I do."

Frustration tightened her grip on the telephone receiver. "Damn it, Roger! I don't want to talk to your mother. I don't want to talk to your secretary. And I don't want to do this on the phone. I'm trying to do the decent thing here, but you're making it damned difficult."

In the pause on the line, Marcy heard only static and the muffled sounds of the busy airport terminal. "You sound upset," Roger said at last.

"We really need to talk. Soon. Can you come over here now?" she asked. After days of rehearsing this in her mind, she was ready to get it over with.

"I would if it weren't for this—"

"Roger, there's not going to be a wedding." The words seemed to burst from her of their own accord. She sat there for a few seconds in shocked silence, then found her voice again. "I'm sorry. I didn't mean to blurt it out over the phone like that."

"Look, if you're not ready to set a date yet—"

"I'm not stalling. I can't marry you."

Again, silence stretched between them. If it weren't for the background noises of the terminal, she'd have thought they'd been cut off. "I remember my sister had prewedding jitters, too," he said at last. "She called the wedding off three times before the big day. Look, I'll probably be tied up until late tonight, but tomorrow evening, let's do something together."

He didn't believe her. Marcy suddenly felt the weight of the world upon her shoulders. He'd been replaced in her heart, and he was too self-assured—or maybe just too stubborn—to understand what she was telling him.

"Why don't you drop by after work? I'll make sandwiches," she said. "I can return your ring then." Better here than somewhere public or, worse yet, at his garage apartment with his parents on the patio below.

"You're not serious?"

"Very," she insisted, although she heard in his answering tone that he still didn't believe her. And she couldn't seem to convince him without telling him about Jack. That was not something to be divulged to a man standing at a pay phone in an airport terminal. She'd already crossed over the line of acceptability, at least in her own mind.

Instead, she simply agreed to have a light dinner ready when he got there the next night, not that she expected either of them to eat it.

An hour later, she was staring blankly at the television, rehearsing what she'd say when he got there. The doorbell rang, startling her, and she jerked, knocking the remote control off the end table.

"Who's there?" she called out, cinching her robe tighter as she stood. He must have finished sooner than he'd expected with the investors.

The sound of Jack's voice, muffled by the door, knocked her senses off balance. She hesitated, then hurried to the door, grinning with a mixture of relief and delight.

She combed her fingers through her still damp hair, took a deep breath, and swung the door open.

His dark eyes glowed with pleasure as he stood there, studying her. She recognized the plaid shirt as

## THE BRIDE'S BEST MAN 109

one she'd given him, and a subtle warmth spread through her. "Hi, stranger," she murmured, feeling suddenly, oddly shy with him.

"Can I come in?" he asked. "I know it's late, and we agreed you'd call when it was time. I was in the neighborhood, though, checking out a job, so I thought I'd drop by for just a minute."

Marcy didn't bother to mask her amusement as she stepped back to let him pass. "What job would you be checking out at this hour?"

"The warehouse refit in the river district. I just got out of a site meeting with the contractor, and I had to pass right by here on the way home," he said.

Funny, he didn't look like he'd just come from a job site. His twill trousers were too crisply pressed, his hair too neatly combed. And he smelled of fresh soap and the woodsy cologne he knew she liked. It wasn't his favorite. It was hers, and he knew it.

Her heart rate increased just a little at the thought. He paused at the kitchen doorway, his gaze sliding back to her face. "You weren't planning on turning in early, were you? If you were, I could just go. I don't want to keep you up."

The comment, as much as the warmth in his appreciative stare, made her aware of the state of her dress. Or undress.

"I'll think I'll change into some jeans or something. I just needed a hot shower to ease some of the tension in my shoulders."

"Rough day?"

"You could say that. Have you eaten yet?" she asked, striving for normalcy.

He nodded. "Sandwiches at the site. I could use something cold to drink, though."

"Me, too." Definitely, she needed something cold and wet to ease the sudden dryness in her throat. That, she decided, could wait until she wore more than a thin old T-shirt and a loosely tied bathrobe. "You know where everything in the kitchen is. Help yourself."

Moments later, she found him on the couch, a glass of lemonade in one hand and the remote control in the other. A second glassful rested on the coffee table, already sweating condensation into one of the cut glass coasters Roger's mother had given her last Christmas.

"Since you haven't called, I'm assuming Roger is still in London," he said as he shifted, settling himself more comfortably on the thick cushions.

"He called a while ago from the airport. I'll return the ring when he comes by here tomorrow evening."

Jack nodded, his expression betraying none of his thoughts. She wondered for an instant if he'd changed his mind, if he regretted kissing her, if he wanted her to stay with Roger and not complicate his own life.

"I told him," she said softly.

"Everything?" Relief shone in his expression, and it occurred to her that perhaps he'd begun to doubt her. Maybe he feared she'd changed her mind.

"Not everything. He was on a pay phone, and it just didn't seem like the right time or place."

Again he nodded, clearly in agreement. "Nobody deserves that. OK, maybe some people do, but neither of us is dumb enough to get engaged to any of them." It was the closest thing to a compliment he'd ever uttered on Roger's behalf, and Marcy suspected it was more a testament to her own good sense than to any of Roger's redeeming qualities.

Her amusement curved into a smile she couldn't quite contain. "If you're not careful, you might actually say something nice about the man."

A shrug lifted Jack's shoulders. "I can't help but feel sorry for the guy. After all, he's losing you."

"And I'm such a prize?"

"For someone like him."

"Meaning?"

"I think I'll let that one alone." Jack propelled a pillow at her head. She ducked sideways, and it bounced off a lamp. She caught the lamp just before it hit the floor.

"That would have cost you," she answered, her eyes wide as she set it upright on the end table. "In fact, I think it's going to cost you anyway." She snatched up the pillow and swung around, landing a blow square on his chest.

He clutched it, preventing her from snatching it back and landing another blow. "How about Saturday at the lake?"

She froze. "What?"

"Saturday. You. Me. Fishing poles. Tackle box. An ice chest full of sandwiches. I'll even make the sandwiches."

"What's that have to do with you nearly breaking my favorite lamp?"

"Why does there have to be a connection? I miss my best buddy—hanging out like this, goofing around, and most of all reeling in a big one with you on the net."

"That most of all, huh?"

With a quick tug on the pillow, he pulled her closer. Her knees bumped against his, and she just managed to keep from tumbling into his lap.

Sparks danced in his stare. "The rest is all new to us, isn't it?"

"Who'd have thought?" she replied, her voice suddenly husky.

He sobered. "I guess that makes the two of us about the densest rocks on the face of the earth, doesn't it?"

"Probably," she agreed, pulling away as the enormity of it all struck her. Her stomach fluttered uncomfortably. Her safe, secure, well-planned future had shattered into a million pieces. There was to be no happily ever after with a wedding cake, a big house, and children—at least not anytime soon.

She wasn't fool enough to expect Jack to walk the path she'd chosen for herself. She knew him too well. He simply didn't believe in love, marriage, and happily ever after. He believed in fun. And sex.

The thought triggered a wave of heat that radiated from her midsection to the tips of her toes and fingers. She turned away, fearing what her expression might reveal. She thought she'd conquered these feelings when she'd conquered the crush she'd developed on Jack at the age of sixteen. She'd never imagined a crush could lay dormant so many years, just waiting for the spark to reignite it.

She snatched up the lemonade and drank it all in big swigs. "Refill?" she asked when she was finished.

# THE BRIDE'S BEST MAN 113

"Chicken."

"Sorry, don't have any," she snapped back, pretending to misunderstand. A well-aimed pillow hit her between the shoulder blades as she stepped through the kitchen doorway.

The doorbell chimed, halting her halfway to the refrigerator. She glanced at the clock, surprised.

"You expecting anyone?" Jack called from the next room.

"No, and it's almost ten."

Jack leaned through the doorway. "Little late to be selling Girl Scout cookies or band candy," he muttered. "I'll see who's there."

"Could be Mrs. Robertson next door. Sometimes she invites me over for a hot toddy before bed."

"And you go?"

"Of course." She added ice cubes to her glass and reached into the fridge for the lemonade.

"It's Roger," Jack called, his tone subdued. She heard the door open, and the two men exchanged stiff greetings. A brief flutter of apprehension quickened her heartbeat. Then she drew a deep breath to calm herself.

With purposeful movements, she crossed to the small countertop desk near the window. Sparing a brief glance outside, she noted Roger's silver Jaguar in one of the guest parking spaces directly under a streetlight. He'd left the top down, darn it. There'd be a scattering of dead bugs on the seats when he left, and he'd hate that.

She wondered if that would trouble him more than what she was about to do.

Carefully, she opened the top drawer and removed

the small manila envelope where the engagement ring now rested. Then she stepped into the next room. The envelope felt heavy in her hand and hot. It might as well have been neon orange the way it drew every pair of eyes in the room.

Jack's gaze shifted after an instant and met hers, steady and warm. "I need to be going. Let me know about Saturday," he said as he backed toward the front door.

She nodded, feeling awkward despite the consideration he exhibited in his speedy exit. "I'll talk to you tomorrow, probably."

She waited until he was gone, then handed the envelope to Roger. He fingered it, and she knew by his expression he recognized the contents by the large bump the ring made in the otherwise smooth surface. Then he set it on the coffee table and sank onto the couch.

"What did Mother do? Or say?"

"Huh?" Confused, Marcy could only stare and wonder what he was talking about. "Surely you don't think I told her before I told you? I may be from a small town, but they do teach us manners there."

"Is that what she said? Marcy, I know she can be a bit of a snob, but you can't let her dictate to you. There are ways to handle her." He stood jerkily and began to pace. "She does mean well."

"She's not the problem," Marcy said quietly. "I am." And so she explained as gently, as kindly as she could manage. Denial deepened the crow's-feet at the corners of his eyes, and he argued, cajoled, and at last lapsed into a cold, angry silence. Still, he

# THE BRIDE'S BEST MAN

seemed unconvinced, even as she ushered him out the door. When he was gone, she noticed he'd left the envelope with the ring in it.

She snatched it off the coffee table and tucked it into her purse. Tomorrow she'd have it delivered by messenger. Maybe then he'd believe she no longer intended to marry him.

A weary tension knotted her shoulders as she sank onto the couch and propped her feet on the coffee table. She reached for the remote, then thought better of it and stretched to reach the portable phone, which still rested on the end table.

She dialed Jack's number, wondering whether he'd be home. It was late, but sometimes when he couldn't sleep he'd go for a run along the riverfront or find a back table in a jazz bar, nurse a single beer through the last set, and then buy a round for the musicians at the end of the night.

Jack answered before the first ring ended. "Marcy?"

"Who else would be calling at this hour—besides Penny the Pincher, that is?"

"Hmm, Penny Pincher. I can't believe I missed that—and now I'll never be able to look at her again without laughing."

Laughter bubbled from her throat. "I can almost guarantee that would cure her of her attraction for you."

"Just what I need. Another woman to hate me. No, thanks. So how did Roger take the news?"

"Not well. He thinks I'm having prewedding jitters."

"Yeah, the permanent kind," Jack responded, then heaved a loud sigh. "I'm sorry I ruined this for you."

Marcy shook her head, then remembered he couldn't see her. "I don't blame you. If anyone's to blame, it's me."

"Don't."

"Don't what?"

"Don't do the guilt thing. It doesn't fix anything. It just gives you a headache, maybe a stomachache, and you miss out on whole lot of fun while you're feeling rotten. And for what? It doesn't solve anything or change anything. Why not just skip the guilt and get on with your life?"

"So speaks the voice of experience." She couldn't help the sarcasm that crept into her tone, or the flicker of sadness his little speech triggered. She'd just made a permanent break with security and a comfortable, companionable future—and for what? A strange passion that had lurked unrecognized beneath the guise of friendship. This passion, this change in her relationship with Jack—it unnerved her. She didn't like uncertainty. She didn't like feeling the earth no longer rested steady beneath her feet.

"Marcy?"

His query startled her from her thoughts, making her realize she'd been silent for some time. "About Saturday," she began, then hesitated.

"You can sleep on it. Let me know tomorrow or the next day," he offered quickly. It struck her that he expected a refusal, that he thought she'd burrow in and wallow in the turmoil of the breakup. Once, she might have done that. She'd changed, though, and he'd been a large part of the cause. He'd upset her sense of reality with that kiss, and she wasn't the same as she'd been.

"What time do you want to pick me up?" she asked.

The early morning air, washed clean from the rain shower they'd driven through, felt cool against Marcy's skin. She set her fishing gear on the bank and gazed out over the lake, shielding her eyes from the rising sun as it broke through a crack in the clouds.

"I've missed this," she murmured, glancing over at Jack. He stood a few feet away, threading fishing line through the eyes on his pole. Glancing up, he flashed her a quick grin, then reached into his tackle box for a hook.

"Well, is it a worm or minnow day?" he asked.

She turned away from the lake and focused on readying her own tackle. "I was hoping you'd loan me that new lure you showed me—the one with the spinners."

"Fat chance."

"Why not? I let you use my trout flies last month."

"They were gathering dust," he retorted.

"And you lost two."

"Which I gave you in the first place, and you know I'll replace them the next time I tie a new batch of flies."

Marcy rocked back on her heels, hiding a smile behind her hand as she faked a yawn. Almost like old times—and how she'd missed these early morning jaunts with Jack. She'd missed the bantering, the comfortable feel of old sneakers and even older jeans, the excitement of casting into the waters and hoping for a big catch.

Fishing, she thought, was a lot like life, especially the hope part. Good equipment and skill mattered, but so much depended on luck.

Her fingers flew as she deftly threaded the fishing line through the guides, then tied on a swivel, the leader, and a snap. The instant he turned, she cautiously reached into his tackle box for the new spinner.

"Just as I thought," he said, turning. "Girls are so sneaky."

"Yeah, and guys are so possessive. What's the matter? Afraid I'll embarrass you?"

"I'll have you know I caught a seventeen-inch bass with that lure just two days ago."

She snapped it onto her line. "Practicing, huh? Afraid I'd make you look bad today?"

"This isn't baseball. Good thing, too, 'cause you hit like a girl."

She rolled her eyes at him as she reached down to flip her tackle boxed closed. "One of life's strange ironies."

She checked the side pocket of her vest for the small jar she'd brought along—her own secret weapon courtesy of the grizzled old angler who ran the bait shop out by the highway. It smelled like something dead, but the old man insisted it drew fish like horse manure drew flies.

"Not that I mind, you being a girl and all," Jack continued, winking provocatively.

# THE BRIDE'S BEST MAN 119

A smirk stole onto her lips. "Took you long enough to notice."

"I noticed," he muttered. "I just tried to take the high road and do the right thing. No sense in ruining a good friendship with sex."

"And now?"

He grinned. "I've reassessed my position."

"About friendship or sex?" She shifted, feeling as uncomfortable as he suddenly looked.

"I am not going to come out ahead in this conversation, so I'd better quit right now before I swallow my foot," he said. "I'm going out on the point," he added, inclining his head toward a spit of land that extended about fifty yards out into the lake.

"Chicken!"

"Bawk! Bawk!" he called out as he strode away. He glanced back and caught Marcy watching him, so he flapped his elbows in a mock chicken dance, nearly dropping his pole in the process.

Marcy's laughter bubbled forth, chasing away the tension that had begun to build between them. She didn't know what lay ahead for them—more awkward moments, probably, and perhaps heartbreak and regrets. She might as well make the most of the present.

Marcy stayed on the bank, fishing a deep hole about a hundred yards from the spit. Within fifteen minutes, thanks to her secret weapon in the jar, she'd landed two keepers. Jack merely gave a dismissive wave when she caught his attention and held them both up on the stringer.

"Sour grapes," she called.

He grimaced, holding a finger to his lips in a signal for silence.

"Yeah, yeah, yeah, quit scaring the fish," she muttered, then stuck her thumbs in her ears, waggled her fingers, and stuck out her tongue at him.

An hour later, she'd landed three more. Jack had abandoned the point in favor of various spots along the bank, where he'd caught a handful of undersized crappie and thrown them back in.

"I'm getting a sandwich. Want one?"

Her stomach rumbled in answer, and she realized she'd skipped breakfast. "I'll be right there." She reeled in her line, secured the lure, and made her way along the narrow path at the edge of the bank until she reached the spot where they'd left their gear. Jack already was rummaging through the deep ice chest he'd hauled down from the car.

"What do we have?" she asked as she leaned her pole against a tree next to his.

"Ham and cheese, egg salad, and our old favorite—"

"—pickles and peanut butter," she finished. "Give me one of those."

He grinned, handing it over. "Soda?" He tossed her a can without waiting for her answer. "I'll take the ice chest. Since you have better padding, you can sit on the rock."

"If I weren't so hungry, I'd slap you for that remark." She brushed a twig from the top of the large, flat stone outcrop, then sat. "What did you wrap this in? Industrial grade shrink wrap?"

He shrugged. "I ran out of the kitchen stuff."

"What are the chances it's food-grade plastic?"

She tugged at a corner, then withdrew a pocketknife from her vest. Grateful she hadn't needed to use it on anything more dirty than new fishing line thus far today, she cut through the plastic that encased her sandwich.

He looked unconcerned. "Don't eat it if you're worried."

"I didn't say I was worried. I was just wondering who to sue if it makes me sick."

"And then who'd tie your trout flies?"

"That you have to replace because you lost my other ones." She tossed the wad of plastic film at him. He caught it easily and tucked it into the ice chest for disposal later. "Thanks for letting me use the spinner." She took a bite, then watched him while she chewed.

"I'm just glad I had a chance to train it properly before you used it," he teased, then grinned widely, knowing good manners would keep her from retorting with a mouthful of his peanut-butter-and-pickles special. It didn't matter what he said. She was the one with all the fish.

Normally when she refused to rise to the bait, he kept teasing and taunting until she retaliated. Now, however, he simply sat there eating his sandwich with exaggerated gusto. "You know," he said after a moment, "this is probably the best peanut-butter-and-pickle sandwich I've eaten in years. Why do you suppose that is?"

"Must be the company," she replied, grinning broadly.

He shook his head. "Nah, I think it's the pickles. I bought a different brand."

"Could be." Her smile didn't slip. She'd bet a month's salary the sparkle she'd glimpsed in his mischievous brown eyes wasn't a trick of the morning sun. He was leading up to something.

He didn't make her wait long. "Nah, it's just the natural glow from a kind, generous act such as sharing that top-notch lure instead of catching all the fish myself. Makes a guy feel good all over."

"And I'm so very grateful," she replied, her tone laced with equal amounts of amusement and sarcasm. At this moment, she could almost believe everything was the same as it had always been between them, that the kiss had never happened. The familiar feel of the banter eased the tight knot that had taken up residence in her midsection.

"In fact," Jack continued, "it's almost better than sex." He stretched his legs out in front of him and heaved a self-satisfied sigh.

*So much for forgetting that kiss.* Marcy pretended to pick a piece of dirt from the corner of her sandwich. "Really?" she said, then frowned at the thready note in her voice.

"It's good in a different kind of pure and unselfish way." His expression remained a study of practiced innocence, the mark of a master prankster.

"Whereas sex isn't pure and unselfish."

He winked, and that innocent expression dissolved into one of potent masculine charm. Marcy blinked once, then again. She couldn't remember him ever looking at her quite like that, and suddenly she understood quite well how he'd managed to beguile all those women for all those years. The effect was staggering.

His slow smile made her insides quiver. "Come on. I'm a guy," he said, with a thread of laughter.

"Yeah, I noticed," she murmured. For a moment, the air felt heavy with promise, with unspoken wishes and unexplored desires. Feeling unsteady, Marcy forced herself to look away. "By the way, you have peanut butter on your chin," she said, forcing the unsteadiness from her voice.

Jack's wry laugh teased her senses. "Jeez, you really know how to spoil the mood." When she didn't respond, he abandoned the ice chest and settled onto the ground beside her.

"So you gave Roger his walking papers, right?"

That was putting it bluntly. "Yes," she answered, then took another bite of her sandwich and tried to ignore how the denim stretched over his thighs and how well shaped those thighs were. It astounded her that she'd never truly noticed before what a beautiful man he was.

No, that wasn't right. She'd noticed. Then she'd put the thought away because it didn't fit their relationship. She'd never wanted to be one of his girls—fun now and discarded later when he got bored or things got a little too serious.

She still didn't want to be just another one of his women.

"You returned the ring?"

"Yes." She didn't explain that she'd had to send it by messenger and when the messenger returned with the ring and a note from Roger, she'd had to send it back again.

"So where does that leave us?" he asked. He

touched her free hand, then twined his fingers with hers.

"We're friends," she said, her voice shaky now.

"And that's all?"

"That's all I know for sure."

"And that's the most important part." Certainty steadied his tone, and she glanced over, meeting his gaze. She saw many things in his eyes, warmth and understanding, patience, and beneath it all, a hint of desire.

"You're my best friend," she said, reminding herself, reminding him, that they were toying with more than a casual date. The stakes were much higher.

Intensity burned in his eyes. "And you're simply the best." The combined effect of those words and that burning stare was devastating. Anything that potent ought to be bottled with a tamperproof cap and a warning label, she decided.

Forcing strength back into her weakened knees, she stood as she slipped the last bite of her sandwich into her mouth. A silent message passed between them, acknowledgment and a decision. For now, the words were enough.

After removing the spinner from her own line, she traded it for the hand-painted lure he'd been using. She recognized it as one he'd made himself, and she took a brief moment to admire the workmanship.

"I like the fins on this one," she replied. "Why just one treble hook instead of two, though?"

"Better balance in the water," he answered. "Not that it makes much of a difference." The heat in his eyes faded as he spoke, and his expression returned to the more familiar wry grin. "I haven't had more than a couple of small nibbles off it today. I wouldn't bother with it if I were you. No sense in screwing up a winning streak."

Her brows lifted in a challenging arch. "Are you implying it's the lure and not my skill?"

"That and a little luck. How else would you explain it?"

The faint flicker of guilt at her trickery vanished at the sight of the smug look on his face. The man was entirely too full of himself. He definitely deserved to be taken down a notch.

"You'll eat those words," she warned him as she picked up her pole. Without a backward glance, she strolled along the bank toward the spot where she'd caught the others. She didn't stop there, but continued several yards further until she stood in the shade of a thick-trunked oak.

She made a great show of checking her line, adjusting the tension on the reel, then casting the lure across the water. After a few moments, she checked to see what Jack was doing. He'd donned his disreputable, broad-brimmed hat and was fishing in a sunny spot near the cooler. Seeing that his attention was occupied, she surreptitiously withdrew the small, flat jar from her pocket and smeared some of the nasty stuff on the lure. She rinsed her hands at the water's edge, sacrificed another towelette, then resumed fishing.

Within an hour, she'd landed three more keepers and thrown back several others. Jack, however, wasn't having much luck. Then again, luck didn't have much to do with it.

After another hour and several more catches, she

took pity on him and joined him. "Try some of this," she said, handing over the jar.

His gaze swiveled between the jar and her face as comprehension dawned across his expression. "You've been using this all along."

She nodded, struggling to choke back a grin. "Gotcha."

He opened the lid, and immediately wrinkled his nose in distaste. "I can't believe I didn't smell it. I can't believe you ate with those hands after touching it."

She withdrew the last foil-wrapped towelette from her pocket and handed it over. His only reply was a surprised grunt. He finished reeling in his lure, then doctored it with the foul-smelling concoction.

His first cast drew a nibble, but he failed to hook his quarry. The second landed near a submerged log with a loud plop. Seconds later, something hit the lure hard. The tip of the pole bent under the strain, and the reel whined.

"I'll get the net," Marcy whispered, already moving in that direction. She grabbed it, then crept back, her attention divided between the slippery path and the battle being waged on the bank ahead. She studied his profile as he played out the line, working the pole, working the fish gradually closer to the bank. He moved with the instinctive grace of a natural athlete, smooth, almost effortless in appearance. The relaxed set of his shoulders and his low whistle seemed at odds with the studied concentration in his expression.

Marcy knew better. Every cell in his body and brain

was focused on that fish, on the fight at hand. At that moment, nothing else in the world mattered.

The observation comforted her. Not everything had changed. Jack still couldn't resist a challenge, and he still poured his entire self into whatever he did and somehow managed to make it look effortless.

"Look at that!" he called out as the fish broke the surface of the water in a frenzy. "Black bass, and he's a big one. Got the net?"

"Right here."

He stepped to the very edge of the water, still working the line. After a moment, he handed her his pole and took the net. "No way am I giving you a chance to let this one get away. One little 'oops, he slipped the hook,' and you'll be crowing for the next year about outfishing me today."

"You think I would do something like that?"

"That's the kind of thing I'd expect out of a cheater. You had this rigged from the beginning."

"I didn't cheat." She gave the pole a vicious tug and reeled in the slack line. Next to her, he bent low, extending the net, ready to scoop up the bass as it neared the water's edge.

"I suppose you'd call it superior technique."

"Actually, yes."

He stretched out, his arm extended, balancing one foot on the bank and another on a rock that cropped through the water's surface at the lake's edge. "Bull hockey! Typical female bull hockey. You sneak around, manipulate, and then pretend to be offended when somebody finds out and calls it what it is. Not that I blame you. After all, you wouldn't stand a chance in a fair contest."

"Really?" Marcy bit her lip, glancing down at his tense, ready position. The picture was simply too tempting. She lifted one booted foot and planted it firmly against his backside. One push was all it took. He tumbled headfirst into the murky water, squealing with outrage.

...ou like steamy passion, mystery and intrigue, ...autiful sophisticated heroines, powerful ...nning heroes, and exotic settings then...

# ZEBRA BOUQUET ROMANCES ARE FOR YOU!

**Special Introductory Offer!**

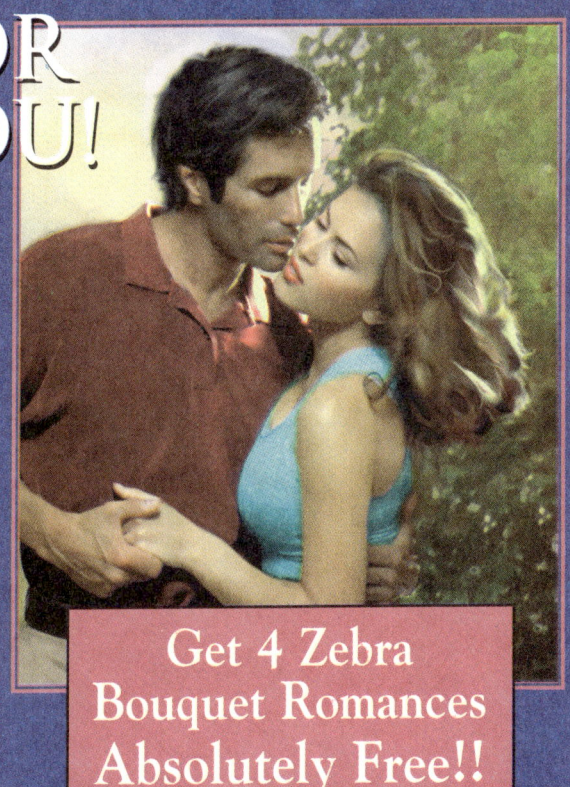

## Get 4 Zebra Bouquet Romances Absolutely Free!!

A $15.96 value - nothing to buy, no obligation

# THE PUBLISHERS OF ZEBRA BOUQUET

are making this special offer to lovers of contemporary romances to introduce this exciting new line of novels. Zebra Bouquet Romances have been praised by critics and authors alike as being of the highest quality and best written romantic fiction available today.

# EACH FULL-LENGTH NOVEL

has been written by authors you know and love as well as by up-and-coming writers that you'll only find with Zebra Bouquet. We'll bring you the newest novels by world famous authors like Vanessa Grant, Judy Gill, Ann Josephson and award winning Suzanne Barrett and Leigh Greenwood—to name just a few. Zebra Bouquet's editors have selected only the very best and highest quality romances for up-and-coming publications under the Bouquet banner.

# YOU'LL BE TREATED

to tales of star-crossed lovers in glamourous settings that are sure to captivate you. These stories will keep you enthralled to the very happy end.

# 4 FREE NOVELS

As a way to introduce you to these terrific romances, the publishers of Bouquet are offering Zebra Romance readers Four Free Bouquet novels. They are yours for the asking with no obligation to buy a single book. Read them at your leisure. We are sure that after you've read these introductory books you'll want more! (If you do not wish to receive any further Bouquet novels, simply write "cancel" on the invoice and return to us within 10 days.)

# SAVE 20% WITH HOME DELIVERY

Each month you'll receive four just-published Bouquet romances. We'll ship them to you as soon as they are printed (you may even get them before the bookstores). You'll have 10 days to preview these exciting novels for Free. If you decide to keep them, you'll be billed the special preferred home subscription price of just $3.20 per book; a total of just $12.80 — that's a savings of 20% off the publisher's price. If for any reason you are not satisfied simply return the novels for full credit, no questions asked. You'll never have to purchase a minimum number of books and you may cancel your subscription at any time.

## GET STARTED TODAY – NO RISK AND NO OBLIGATION

To get your introductory gift of 4 Free Bouquet Romances fill out and mail the enclosed Free Book Certificate today. We'll ship your free books as soon as we receive this information. Remember that you are under no obligation. This is a risk-free offer from the publishers of Zebra Bouquet Romances.

**Call us TOLL FREE at 1-888-345-BOOK**
**Visit our website at www.kensingtonbooks.com**

---

## FREE BOOK CERTIFICATE

**YES!** I would like to take you up on your offer. Please send me 4 Free Bouquet Romance Novels as my introductory gift. I understand that unless I tell you otherwise, I will then receive the 4 newest Bouquet novels to preview each month FREE for 10 days. If I decide to keep them I'll pay the preferred home subscriber's price of just $3.20 each (a total of only $12.80) plus $1.50 for shipping and handling. That's a 20% savings off the publisher's price. I understand that I may return any shipment for full credit-no questions asked-and I may cancel this subscription at any time with no obligation. Regardless of what I decide to do, the 4 Free Introductory Novels are mine to keep as Bouquet's gift.

BN070A

Name _____

Address _____

City _____ State _____ Zip _____

Telephone ( ) _____

Signature _____
(If under 18, parent or guardian must sign.)

Orders subject to acceptance by Zebra Home Subscription Service. Terms and Prices subject to change.
Order valid only in the U.S.

**If this response card is missing, call us at 1-888-345-BOOK.**

**Be sure to visit our website at www.kensingtonbooks.com**

**BOUQUET ROMANCES**
Zebra Home Subscription Service, Inc.
P.O. Box 5214
Clifton NJ 07015-5214

PLACE STAMP HERE

# SEVEN

Jack burst upward through the surface of the water with a splash nearly as great as the one he'd made when he fell in. The pole rose from the water next, still tightly gripped in his right hand. Sputtering, cursing, he twisted around and glared at Marcy. Surprise mingled with the anger in his expression.

"Why did you do that?" he roared.

"I'm sorry," she said, trying to stifle a giggle. "You bent over, and I couldn't help myself."

"I damn near lost my fish," he growled as he shifted, finding his footing on the muddy lake bottom. The water lapped about his waist, and he backed up a step, fighting for lost ground with the fish. "Give me the net!"

She extended one arm, balancing the net over the water with a light, careful grip. With a sudden jerk, he tugged it toward him with his free hand. Disappointment flickered in his expression when she let go easily, without a single slip toward the water. "Thought you'd pull me in with you, huh?"

He grunted, his gaze back on the ripple where his catch waited, its fins fluttering in the water as it tested its tether, then changed direction for another attempt at escape. "It was worth a try," he said as he tucked the net handle under one arm and began to reel in the line. "Don't worry, though. I'll get even later."

"You'll try."

"Maybe not today, maybe not tomorrow, but when you least expect it—that's when I'll get you," he said. He shifted until he held the pole in one hand and the net in the other. With quick, skillful movements, he netted the fish.

He turned around, his face a picture of satisfaction. "Now that's a fish and a half," he said, lifting the net enough for her to see the size of his catch.

She applauded her approval.

"You'll pardon me if I skip the bow," he replied. "I've already swallowed enough lake water today."

Laughter bubbled through her, mingling with an odd mixture of relief, delight, and something that felt very much like contentment. Roger would have grumbled for a month if she'd shoved him into the lake headfirst—not that she'd ever have considered doing such a thing, even if she'd ever managed to convince him to stand that close to the muddy edge.

Jack, though, never minded when she got the best of him. He could take a joke as well as he could deliver one. It was a quality she hadn't sufficiently appreciated until now.

"You know, you could've drowned me," he remarked as he stepped closer, splashing almost as much with each step as the fish flipping against the confines of the net.

"In three feet of water? Come on."

"There's a steep drop-off a few feet out," he reminded her. "You've seen charts. What if I'd slipped off there?"

She heaved an exaggerated sigh. "I guess I'd have been forced to rescue you."

He waggled his eyebrows. "And give me mouth-to-mouth?"

"CPR? I doubt that would be called for."

"You'd just let me die?"

"You swim like a fish," she retorted as he extended the pole toward her. She took it from him carefully, holding it steady while he unhooked the fish and let it drop back into the net.

Jack hooked the lure on one of the pole guides. Then, when Marcy expected him to release his end of the pole, he gave a sharp jerk instead. Instinctively, Marcy's fingers tightened, and she slid forward in the mud. Off balance, she teetered on one foot, struggling to remain upright. Then, in what felt like a slow-motion replay, she tipped toward Jack—toward the rippled surface of the lake.

For an instant, it looked like he might catch her. "Gotcha," he shouted, a wide grin spreading from ear to ear. "Payback time!" He stepped back, letting her splash into the lake beside him.

She caught herself before she went completely under, turning her tumble into an awkward dog paddle. Her waterlogged shoes pulled her feet down, acting like sinkers as she tried to tread water at the edge of the shelf he'd reminded her of just a few minutes earlier. She kicked hard, and with a few strokes was back in shallow water.

"OK, we're even," she acknowledged as she struggled to stand on the moss-slick lake bottom. No wonder he'd had such a hard time. She'd had less trouble walking on ice last winter than she was having now.

"Not quite," Jack replied, stepping nearer. He still balanced the net in one hand, but he barely seemed to notice the continued struggles of his catch. All his attention focused on Marcy, and there was a mischievous gleam in his eyes.

Too late, she realized what he meant to do. She took a step backward, then felt his foot hook behind her ankle. At the same time, he pushed against her shoulder, dunking her beneath the surface.

She caught a fistful of his shirt, pulling him down with her. Holding her breath, Marcy squirmed sideways. She bumped against the net, felt the prick of the sharp fins, and shifted directions. The murky water swirled around her as she spun away from Jack, kicking free of the net, which had tangled around her foot.

Seconds later, she burst to the surface, sputtering with indignation. Jack came up a few feet away, his hands empty, his expression dumbfounded. He blew a mouthful of muddy water into the air, then groaned. "The biggest darned bass I ever caught, and you let it get away."

"*I* let it get away? I don't think so."

"You're right." He stood and slicked his hair back from his face with one hand. "You're absolutely right. You didn't *let* it get away. You turned it loose!"

Marcy backpedaled, putting more distance between herself and the gleam that had returned to his brown eyes. "Funny, that's not how I remember it."

"Hmmph!" Instead of chasing after her to dunk

her again, as she expected, he moved in a slow circle, shuffling in an odd gait.

"What are you doing?"

"Looking for the pole."

She'd forgotten about that. Spotting the net floating a few yards away, she waded over to retrieve it. Then she carefully made her way to the bank and tossed it into the grass. Seeing that Jack hadn't yet located his fishing rod, which she knew to be a quite nice and expensive one, she decided she'd better help him.

His expression clouded, he gazed into the murky water. If she didn't know better, she'd have thought he could see straight to the bottom, so intense was his concentration. They'd stirred up so much silt, though, that she couldn't see her own hand just inches beneath the surface. Unless he'd developed X-ray vision in the last few minutes, he couldn't see, either, but that didn't stop him from staring downward as though he could.

Maybe he was trying to will the pole to come to him. The thought triggered a giggle, which earned her a stone-faced glare. "Just for the record, this is all your fault," she reminded him. She hoped the fishing rod hadn't slid into the deep hole beyond the shelf and that neither of them kicked it there as they searched.

It would be easier if they were barefooted, but she wasn't stupid enough to risk stepping on Jack's lure or any other lost or discarded hook that happened to be lurking on the bottom. Her right foot bumped against something, and she shifted, thinking it was another rock. Then she felt the length of the pole, lying like a stick across her path.

"I think I found it," she called out. She crouched down, keeping her head just above water. She couldn't quite reach it, even when she stretched her fingertips. Jack stood a few yards away, his expression hopeful.

"I thought I found it twice, too, but they were just sticks," he said.

"Nope, this is it." She tried without success to flick the pole upward with the tip of her shoe. "Aw, what the heck, I'm already as wet and dirty as I'm going to get." She clamped her mouth closed and plunged downward, feeling gingerly along the bottom until her fingers closed around the pole.

She stood and let out a triumphant whoop. She lifted the pole aloft and grinned. "Guess we're not even anymore," she taunted. "Mister, you owe me one big debt of gratitude."

He strode closer, moving with purposeful ease through the water. Funny, he seemed to be having absolutely no trouble maneuvering now, but maybe that was because they'd already stirred loose all the silt and moss that had made the bottom so slippery.

"You are a goddess," he told her.

"You just realized that?" she teased. Even with his hair plastered against his head and muddy water dripping from his arms, he looked like every woman's fantasy, sprung from the depths. Poseidon in a faded blue T-shirt.

His gaze held hers, his eyes as warm as the sun beating down on her back. He drew a deep breath as he stopped a few feet away, and his gaze dipped slightly. Heat flared in the depth of his eyes, and suddenly she was aware of her own wet clothing plastered to her body.

She wore only a light cotton shirt with a thin bra beneath it. A shiver traveled up her spine, and she could feel her nipples beading against the thin fabric. She might as well be naked.

Turning, she headed for the bank. In her hurry, she slipped. Jack caught her from behind, circling her waist as he steadied her. The heat of his touch burned through the thin shirt, and she felt weak in the knees.

"Thanks," she managed.

He didn't answer. Instead, she felt his lips at the nape of her neck. Shock stole her breath—shock at his unexpected kiss and shock at her own reaction. Desire, hot and immediate, flashed through her. She couldn't think, couldn't move her feet another step. Her head lolled to one side, allowing him easier access, and he took full advantage. He kissed a path from her nape to the hollow behind her ear, then turned her in his arms.

He took the pole from her slack fingers and tossed it onto the bank. His arms encircled her and his lips closed on hers, possessive and demanding. The sun shining down on her hair seemed cool compared with the heat flaring between them.

His tongue brushed against her teeth, and she opened her mouth, teasing and withdrawing. She knew this game, but she'd never played it with him before. Never dreamed of it. Never dared. And never in a million years would she have imagined standing under the hot summer sun, waist deep in water, kissing Jack in broad daylight for anyone to see.

Warm sunshine. Warm skin. Hands at her back. Lips at her throat. The evidence of his desire pressed against her. Her own desire tautened her breasts, pulling the tips into hard, aching knots.

A sense of wonder laced through Marcy's growing need. Jack, her best friend, was setting her on fire. If it weren't for the fact she stood in water to her waist, she thought she might spontaneously combust.

She recognized the sensations, but they'd never held such power before. They'd never struck with such intensity. She wondered how she'd managed to go so many years not realizing what was beneath her nose.

Jack.

He knew how to punch all her buttons.

He knew her better than anyone. He knew what made her laugh, what made her cry. He knew how to tease a smile through her tears and how to make her forget her troubles.

And now he wanted her—wanted her in the most elemental way a man could want a woman. She wanted him, too. Right here, right now, she could admit that, at least to herself.

But for how long? And at what cost?

The thought was a sour note in the harmony of the moment, and she thrust it away. Instead, she concentrated on the feel of his damp hair between her fingers, the sensuous touch of his hand at her waist, sliding beneath the hem of her shirt.

His fingers crept upward, then halted. He lifted his head, and a wry grin crinkled the corners of his mouth. "Maybe we do need to rent a room," he whispered.

Suddenly self-conscious, Marcy glanced around them. Two gray-haired men fished from a small boat a hundred yards offshore, studiously ignoring them. A high-pitched, off-key whistle drifted over the water, followed by the low murmur of voices. Farther down the shoreline, a small boy tossed rocks in the water while two older children openly stared.

Marcy groaned and pulled away. "I've lost my mind. I've definitely lost my mind. Necking in public, for heaven's sake." She turned, trudging up the steep incline, out of the water, and onto the bank. She flopped down on the rock outcropping and kicked off her sodden shoes. He took the pole from her.

"Our mothers would be shocked," she muttered as Jack joined her on the rock. His nearness reignited the heat that had barely begun to cool.

"Our mothers seem to be reexperiencing puberty," he replied.

A low chuckle bubbled up from her chest. "What is the world coming to? The next thing you know, we'll see pigs flying out there with the Canadian geese," she said with a distracted wave of her hand toward the lake, where a pair of geese swooped low over the water, heading for the opposite shore.

"Look! There goes one now!"

She elbowed him in the ribs, nudging him off the rock onto the mud. "You're so full of yourself."

"And you like it," he challenged.

She stared at her mud-brown socks, which had been a pristine white when she put them on this morning. "Maybe," she admitted. "You do have certain attributes."

"Such as?"

"I think you've fished enough for one day." She pushed herself upright and stepped gingerly through the knee-high grass toward the cooler. "Swimming always makes me hungry. How about you?"

Surprised by his burst of laughter, she glanced back over her shoulder. "What?"

"Marcy, darling, you have a gift for the double *entendre*."

She squinted, shading her eyes from the sun as she studied his face. For the life of her, she couldn't figure out what she'd said that could be construed as having a double meaning.

"Hungry? Yes, I'd say I'm hungry," he said, his tone thick with meaning. Her heated flush arose as much from the look in his eyes as from the sudden understanding of what she'd said and what he'd inferred. "I'll take one of those sandwiches, and just about anything else you're willing to offer," he added.

Unable to speak past the thick knot in her throat, Marcy knelt next to the cooler and flipped the lid open. She wanted to lean over it and fan the cool air over her face, anything to ease the uncomfortable flush on her face—heck, the heat had spread clear to the tips of her toes.

Feeling Jack's gaze on her, she simply reached inside and pulled out two sandwiches. Turning, she tossed one toward him. He caught it easily and grinned. "Jackpot! The last peanut-butter-and-pickle sandwich."

Marcy didn't mind. She figured she'd had enough pleasure for one day. Any more excitement and she'd be in danger of heart failure—or spontaneous combustion, now that she was out of the water.

Marcy spent the next week fending off Roger's attempts at reconciliation and trying not to make a complete fool of herself over Jack.

"You realize, of course, this could be nothing more than a rebound romance," she told him one night as he kissed her good night after an evening of pizza and rented movies.

He shook his head. "That's when you're the dumpee, not the dumper."

The next evening, she worried what she'd do for a best friend now that he'd inserted himself into the role of boyfriend.

"Boyfriend, best friend." He shrugged. "What more could you need?" A shadow danced behind the smile in his eyes when he spoke, though, and for a long time they both remained silent. Jack stared out the window at the children playing in the park across the street and she stared at him.

His expression confused her. Slightly sad, slightly wistful, and so very serious, he looked unlike the Jack she'd always known. He was much more complicated than she'd given him credit for, and she wondered what he was thinking. She didn't ask, though. He'd tell her when and if he was ready, and until then he'd simply joke his way around the issue.

The following Saturday, Marcy had to work until six to smooth out a glitch in the system of one of her better customers. She arrived home, exhausted and tense, to find Jack sitting on the front steps of her building with bags of Chinese food beside him.

The day's tension seeped away at the sight, and she grinned. "I just love a man who can cook," she teased.

"I aim to please, ma'am." He lifted the bags, clearing the way for her to pass, then followed her inside to the elevator. The presence of an elderly couple forced him to behave himself while they waited for the elevator and for the first two floors of the ride. When the doors closed behind the departing couple, leaving the two of them alone, he leaned close, kissing her soundly on the lips. He reached around her, still holding one bag, and somehow managed to pinch her behind.

She squealed and jumped sideways. "Behave yourself."

"Why? I have a lot of lost time to make up for," he teased.

Her eyebrows arched in amusement. "And whose fault is that?"

"I could blame it on a lot of things," he said. "But I suspect we both had a lot of practicing to do before we got around to what was right."

"You got a lot more practice than me."

"Evidently I needed it." That sly grin she recognized as a sign of trouble to come stole onto his face. "I think I still need it. You could give me lessons."

The doors opened on her floor, and she stepped out. "In your dreams, buddy," she taunted.

"Every night, baby. Every night." He caught up with her and planted a kiss at the nape of her neck, right at the most sensitive point. A soft gasp escaped her lips, followed by a sharp intake of breath as she spotted Mrs. Robertson from the next apartment watering the plants in the atrium.

"Behave yourself," she whispered, smiling in spite of her embarrassment. "We're in a public place, and I have to live here and face these people."

"Good afternoon, Mrs. Robertson," he said as they passed.

"You again?" the older woman replied, her lined face crinkling into a grin. "What's for dinner?"

"Chinese. Want to join us?" he offered.

Mrs. Robertson beamed her pleasure. "Thank you so much for the offer, but I've already eaten. Maybe you'll join me for a cup of tea later."

"That would be nice," Marcy answered. "Wouldn't it, Jack?"

His smile widened. "I do enjoy your tea, Mrs. Robertson," he said. "It packs quite a punch."

"I'll just knock on the wall when it's ready," she said. "And this time I'll knock loud so you can hear me if you're busy."

Marcy turned to hide the flush she felt spreading up her neck and across her face. She pretended to fumble with her door key, remembering Mrs. Robertson's consternation two nights ago when they'd been too wrapped up in another of those mind-drugging kisses to hear the poor woman's knocking. Jack had made some excuse while Marcy had tried to pull her thoughts together. Marcy wondered whether Mrs. Robertson really believed him or was simply good at hiding her suspicions.

Jack was still chatting with Mrs. Robertson when

Marcy unlocked the door. She set her briefcase on the hall table, then retreated to her bedroom to change into an old pair of jeans and a comfortable T-shirt. By the time she was finished, Jack was in the kitchen, setting the table with paper plates, chopsticks, and the brass candlesticks with the ivory tapers from the fireplace mantle.

"That's an interesting mix. Are we celebrating or expecting a power outage?" She leaned against the doorjamb, her arms crossed as she watched him unpack the bags from the restaurant. "And are we expecting guests?" He'd brought enough food to feed a dozen people.

"I look better by candlelight," he answered. "And no, I didn't invite anyone but Mrs. Robertson. Since she declined, I guess it's just you and me. We won't have to leave the apartment for days."

His broad wink triggered a brief laugh. "And now who's king of the double *entendre?* You are incorrigible. I don't know how I've put up with you all these years."

"Must be my good looks, keen intelligence, and food-gathering skills."

"You definitely have a talent for providing food," she admitted. She languidly pushed herself away from the doorjamb and ambled toward the table. He had many other talents, too, some of which she'd only recently experienced. All these years, she'd suspected—no, she'd known—he was a man of monumental charm and allure. She hadn't realized how potent that charm could be until he'd directed it fully at her. Before that night at the Rose Festival, he'd never done so.

# THE BRIDE'S BEST MAN 143

She wasn't sure why he'd done so, why he'd forced this changed in their friendship. It was a complication, and she couldn't foresee where it would lead or how it would end. All she could do was enjoy the present and try not to lose her head. And she certainly was enjoying the present.

After dinner, they moved to the balcony to watch the sunset and the people in the park and the squirrels in the trees. They talked about his day, her day, their respective neighbors, and the fishing prospects for the coming weeks. As the sky darkened, their conversation dwindled to an occasional comment breaking long spells of comfortable silence.

Marcy's thoughts drifted back through the years to other comfortable silences. She'd always been at ease with him, maybe because there'd been no pressure, no standard to live up to, and no image to uphold. Was that why she was so attracted to him now? Was it simply that she didn't have to prove herself with him?

No, it had to be more than that. If she were honest with herself, the attraction had always been there, simmering beneath the surface. She'd just refused to acknowledge it, refused to take it seriously. How could she when they wanted such different things, when he turned everything serious into a joke and teased her out of any serious thought she might have?

How could she acknowledge it now?

The question taunted her, and she had no answer. Before she could dwell on it for long, though, Jack scooted his chair closer and wrapped his hand around hers. "Want to rent a movie?"

"Do you?"

"This is nice," he replied. "But if you're bored, we can do something."

She smiled in the darkness. "I'm never bored with you." It was true, she realized. When they were together, he filled her world. She never knew quite what he'd say or do next. She knew him better than anyone else in this world, but still he surprised her. And even when he was silent, she still felt his presence and was happy because he was there.

Heavens, she'd be a rich woman if she could bottle that quality and sell it. But she couldn't even name it. She just knew whatever it was, he had it.

She leaned across the arm of the chair and kissed him, surprising him. She could tell by his sharp intake of breath he hadn't expected her to kiss him, not just yet. Pleasure spread through her, partly from the kiss and partly because she could still surprise him, too. Maybe he wouldn't become bored with her, either, at least not for a good long while.

He shifted then, tugging her out of her chair and into his lap. She was grateful she'd sprung for the sturdy, well-built wooden loungers instead of the lighter ones she'd been considering because of their clean, elegant lines. She'd take clunky and sturdy over fragile elegance any night.

Marcy lost track of time as they kissed and touched and explored the newness between them. Then lights flashed across the balcony, and awareness returned.

"Maybe we should go inside," she suggested, then slapped at a mosquito. "No, we definitely should go inside."

"And what?"

She shrugged in the darkness. "Whatever. I just

don't want to spend the next week covered in calamine lotion." She tugged his hand, pulling him up from the chair.

"I could go home now," he said, then pulled her against him. "Or stay. It's up to you to set the pace, to say yes or no."

She tipped her face upward, studying him in the moonlight. Desire shone in his eyes, but it was a patient, contained desire. He wouldn't push her, wouldn't make demands she wasn't ready to answer. She could trust him, oddly, and that was because he'd proven himself time and again through all the years they'd grown up together, through all that had happened since they'd become adults.

But could she trust herself? Could she take what he offered and not want more, not demand more? Could she simply accept what they had, then move on when the time came?

She kissed him softly, hoping she had the courage to let go when the time came. He wasn't a man to be constrained by conventions, to be boxed into the confines of marriage, children, a mortgage, and all the trappings such a life entailed. It didn't fit him, and he didn't believe in the basic concept.

She was, however, a mature woman now, seasoned by love and loss, even though the most recent loss had been more of illusions than true heartbreak. She could be who she needed to be, and when the time came, she could become simply his good friend once more.

At least that's what she hoped.

Their kiss deepened, and she pressed against him, feeling the evidence of his own burgeoning desire.

A wild joy fluttered within her. Tonight, she thought. Tonight she'd break free of the bonds of convention. Tonight she'd be a woman of the moment, would live life on his terms, would love on his terms.

Headlights flashed again across the balcony. Then a voice intruded from below, clear and familiar.

"Good Lord, Marcy, what the hell are you doing?"

# EIGHT

"Roger?" Marcy stared at the figure standing on the sidewalk below them. A nearby street light illuminated his pale expression. "What are you doing here?"

"You and Jack? I didn't think—it never occurred to me . . ." Shock tightened his features into a stiff mask.

*Roger here? Now?* Her mind, still befuddled by that toe-curling kiss, struggled with a jumble of disconnected thoughts. His unexpected appearance. The mist from the automatic sprinklers dampening the sidewalk—dampening his shoes. The glittering lights of the city twinkling all around them. The yellow glow of the bug light outside the apartment below. Roger. Jack's stiff, protective stance, his arm looping around her waist, holding her against him. Roger's tuxedo. The paper grocery sack he was holding.

"Why are you wearing a tuxedo?" she asked. It wasn't the most important question, just the most puzzling. She searched her memory for some event they'd been scheduled to attend together, something she'd left unclear when she'd returned his ring or during the numerous phone calls he'd made to her since then.

No, she'd been quite clear. The engagement was over, and she thought it best for all concerned that they make a clean break of it. It would be easier if they didn't see one another, at least for a while. He'd agreed.

At least that's what she'd thought.

Shifting the sack, Roger glared up at them. "I brought back a few things you left at my apartment."

"I—I—" Marcy drew a deep breath, trying to shake off the awkwardness. "Why don't you come up?" she finally managed as she slid a step sideways. Jack released her without protest and backed into the shadows.

"You want me to go?" he asked after Roger disappeared through the back entrance to the building.

She shook her head. "Not unless you want to. I know this is awkward."

Sympathy softened his expression. "More for you than for me." He tilted his head to one side and rubbed his chin thoughtfully. "You didn't tell him about us?"

She took a deep breath. "Maybe I should have. I just didn't see the need, and I figured it would make a bad situation worse."

"Probably." He stuffed his hands in his pockets and leaned back against the wall. "I kind of feel sorry for the guy. After all, he lost out on a pretty good thing."

She hesitated on her way inside, one hand on the door, the other going to her hip. "So that's what I am to you—a pretty good thing?" she challenged.

In the semidarkness, she could just make out the hint of a smile in his expression. "The best," he said, and looked as though he might have said more if Roger's knock hadn't come at that moment.

Jack dropped a light kiss on her forehead. "I'll wait out here. I don't imagine I'm his favorite person right now. No sense in adding insult to injury."

She nodded her agreement and reached for the screen. "Thank you," she murmured, then hurried inside.

Roger's fist was poised to knock again when Marcy swung the front door open. "There you are. I thought maybe you hadn't heard." A touch of sarcasm tainted his tone, and his lips curved into an unpleasant smile.

"I heard," she answered, not wanting to elaborate. "We were just debating why you dressed up to deliver a paper sack full of my stuff."

"I'm sure," he said, his tone disbelieving.

He composed his expression into the dignified mask he used to hide his real feelings, whatever they might be. The mask couldn't quite hide the anger in his eyes. He stepped past her into the apartment, his footsteps echoing on the tiled floor of the hallway.

"I'm sorry," Marcy told him. She twisted her fingers awkwardly together as she followed him into the kitchen.

"Apparently I should have called," Roger said. He'd set the bag on the table and was patting his jacket pockets. "I was almost out the door when I remembered the earrings. I know they're here somewhere. The braised copper ones you bought at the street fair."

"They're heavy." She remembered taking them off in his kitchen while she made sandwiches one evening. Heavy and uncomfortable after a few hours' wear. And a bit tacky, Roger had thought at the time. She was surprised he hadn't tossed them into the trash when he found them.

"Ah, there they are." He removed them from an inside pocket and made a halfhearted attempt to untangle the ear wires from the dangling beads and copper chains he'd found so unappealing.

"I'll do that later," she said, taking them from him. She set the earrings next to the bag, then absently stroked the grain of the oak tabletop, wondering why he just stood there, staring at her, his expression unreadable.

"I was hoping we could talk, but I suppose this isn't a good time." He winced, then loosened his tie as he continued. "How long have you been playing me for a fool, Marcy?"

She heard the balcony screen slide open, followed by Jack's footsteps on the parquet flooring. "You know me better than that," she retorted. "Have you been drinking?"

He shrugged, then turned and leaned on the sink. "A glass of champagne during intermission. I've been to the symphony with some of my associates from the office. The performance was a fund-raiser for Children's Mercy Hospital. Very nice," he said, his tone distracted.

It was something they would have done together if she hadn't broken their engagement, an evening she probably would have enjoyed. She felt no regret at having missed it, though, only that he'd been witness to what must have been for him a painful display.

"Several of our friends asked about you." He turned, facing her now, his brows knit together in puzzlement.

*His friends. They'd accepted her because of him, not because she fit in.* Maybe she eventually would have been comfortable with that crowd, but that was a moot point under the circumstances.

"I was thinking of you as I drove home," Roger continued. "It seems, however, you have not missed me as much as I would have hoped." Pain registered briefly in his expression before he shuttered the emotion behind a pale, dignified smile. He took a drink from the glass he'd just filled.

"You should have called," she said softly. A chill from the air-conditioning vents or the emotional turmoil of the moment, she wasn't sure which, raised goose bumps on her arms, chasing away the last traces of heat from Jack's kiss. A niggling sense of unease, of some point that didn't fit the whole picture, teased at the edge of her awareness, but she couldn't grasp anything specific.

"Yes, I should have called. It just never occurred to me that you would be . . . otherwise occupied. Working, perhaps, but not . . . not . . ." He shook his head, as if trying to dislodge the mental picture. "Him?"

She heard Jack come into the kitchen, and she frowned over her shoulder at him. His brief smile, meant only for her, eased the knot of tension building at the base of her neck.

"Good to see you again, Roger," he said, his tone noncommittal.

"I'm sorry I can't say the same," Roger replied. He glanced out the kitchen window briefly, and pursed his lips together with distaste as his gaze returned to her. Then he slid past her. "Jack, we've never gotten on well, but I did believe you always had Marcy's best interests at heart. I hadn't expected you to take advantage of her when she's vulnerable."

Marcy winced at the condemnation in Roger's voice. "It's not like that," she began.

Jack's hand tightened possessively on her arm, halting her words. "I don't think you have a clue about Marcy's best interests."

"And you do?" His brows lifted in a disbelieving arch.

"As a matter of fact, I do."

Roger laughed, sounding genuinely amused. The smile didn't extend past his lips. "And I'm supposed to believe you can make her happier than I can, that you will marry her and provide a large, beautiful home, children, a luxury sedan, and the respect of the community?"

"I won't try to turn her into someone she isn't meant to be. I think she's just fine already—too good for the Ashforths, actually."

Marcy glanced from one to the other. "I'm standing right here."

Roger continued as if she hadn't spoken. "The Ashforth name means something in this state."

"Yep, I guess it does," Jack replied in a less than complimentary tone. "I wouldn't be bragging about it to *real* folks, though."

"Meaning?"

"I thought my meaning was pretty clear. Having trouble? Maybe that's why you can't really understand what it is Marcy needs from a man."

"A real man wouldn't toy with her feelings."

Marcy's irritation deepened to anger. She'd heard enough of this ridiculous posturing. "OK, boys. Tuck the testosterone back in your pockets before I throw you both out of here."

The two men glared at each other for a moment. Then Roger's derisive laughter cut through the silence. "Some best friend you are. Breaking up her engagement, taking advantage in a vulnerable time—"

"That engagement needed breaking up."

"That's enough," Marcy said, stepping between the two men. The word *vulnerable* had passed Roger's lips one time too many. "Roger, thank you for returning my things. I think it's time for you to go home."

"Marcy, I—"

"No, not another word. Not tonight," she interrupted, stepping around him. "This discussion is over."

"Some discussion," Jack muttered, and she shot him a warning look over her shoulder. Roger followed her to the front door, which she had open by the time he reached it.

"Just for the record," she said as he stepped into the hallway, "I didn't ask you to leave so Jack could continue to take advantage of me during this *vulnerable* time. You talked about me like I wasn't even there, like I was a little kid with cottage cheese for brains. I was standing right there, for heaven's sake."

He looked startled. "I didn't realize. I mean, you didn't think I—" His handsome face stared down at her, confusion clouding his blue eyes. "I'm just concerned about you."

"Don't make it worse, Roger. Just go."

He hesitated, looking as if he wanted to say more. Then he clamped his jaw shut and turned toward the stairs. With a sigh of frustration, Marcy swung the door closed.

Jack stood in the hallway, wishing he knew how to erase the troubled lines that creased her forehead. She strode toward him, rubbing at her temples.

"Headache?" He reached out to pull her into his arms, but she held back, her body stiff.

"Two," she answered. Her small white teeth worried at a fingernail.

"Stop that!" he said, catching her hand. "You quit chewing your nails ten years ago."

She glared up at him. "Yeah? Well, I feel like starting now. You got a problem with that?"

He held up both hands in a gesture of surrender. "Hey, I'm not the enemy here."

She glared up at him. "What did you mean by that remark—that my engagement needed breaking up?"

To his consternation, he felt a guilty flush travel up his neck. Hoping she wouldn't notice, he forced himself to meet her irate stare. "I want you to be happy. You know that."

She crossed her arms tightly across her chest. The movement lifted her small breasts, but he refused to let himself react. He wanted to throw her on the couch and kiss away the doubts flickering in those beautiful brown eyes, to convince her he'd sell his soul to keep unhappiness from touching her. He figured she'd probably slug him in the gut if he tried.

"Did you decide to break up my engagement—for my own good, of course? Is that what that kiss was all about?"

"Which kiss?" He realized the second the words left his mouth he'd screwed up. Hot anger snapped in every movement as she stomped toward the door. "Wait! That didn't come out right."

She spun around. "Did you deliberately set out to ruin my relationship with Roger? Is that what all of this was about? You decided to be a *good* friend and save me from myself?" Hurt mingled with the fury in her expression, a lethal combination in his experience. Pain shot through him at the knowledge of the hurt he'd unintentionally inflicted.

"I care about you."

"Yeah, I know you do." She closed her eyes and drew a deep breath, as if to calm herself.

The knot in the pit of his stomach eased. For a second. Just long enough for him to think she might understand what he meant, how it had happened for him. "I'd do anything for you."

"Even pretend to have the hots for me. Anything to keep me from wasting my life on Roger, right?" She reached behind her and opened the door. "I think you should go, too."

He didn't move. "I didn't pretend."

Her tight smirk reflected her skepticism. "Oh, that's right. I forgot. You're Jack Rathert, superstud, and I am, after all, a healthy, red-blooded female with all the right parts, even if some of them aren't as extraordinary as what you're accustomed to."

"I think you're the next best thing to perfect. Always have."

Again, she crossed her arms defensively. "In a platonic sort of way."

"The other was there. I just knew better than to mess with a good thing. Plus, we didn't fit that way. We wanted different things. Maybe we still do, but you have to admit we fit a lot better than you and Roger. I just had to make you see that."

His words had little effect on her anger, though. If anything, he'd only made things worse, judging from her expression.

"Do you have a clue how insulting that sounds? And what a cliché it is? Neanderthals. You're all Neanderthals. You might be out of the cave, but you're still treating us like we're incapable of taking care of ourselves."

He drew a deep breath. "Maybe you're right. I should go now." He hesitated in the doorway. "I've been a dense, blind idiot for a long time. Maybe a little stupid, too. But that kiss was real, and so was every kiss since then. It's all very, very real, and so are my feelings for you."

A brick wall would have been more accepting than Marcy was at that moment. He could see it in the tense set of her shoulders, the stubborn tilt of her chin. "Just go, Jack."

He nodded slowly and did as she asked. Maybe in a day or two, maybe a week, she'd be ready to listen to him. Until then, he'd be wasting his breath.

She slammed the door closed before he'd gone three steps. The sound cut through him like a knife, leaving a chilled place where his heart used to be.

# THE BRIDE'S BEST MAN 157

He'd taken a risk, played the odds. For a while, it looked like it might pay off. Now, who could guess?

An hour later, Jack found himself standing outside The Corner Spot. The bar and grill occupied the northwest corner of the main intersection in Oldtown, a quaint old business district that was undergoing a revival. Good food. Good beer. Good music. He'd spent a lot of evenings here with Marcy.

The couple at the window table reminded him of the two of them, not because of how they looked, but because they seemed so comfortable together. The man said something, and the woman tipped her head back, laughing. Then she leaned close and whispered something, and they both laughed harder.

How many times had he and Marcy sat there, laughing, teasing, her tossing a crumpled napkin at him in retaliation for some comment he'd tossed off?

"Hey, Jack! Good to see you," one of the waiters called out. "There's a table free in the back."

"Thanks, but it's just me tonight. I'll sit at the bar." He chose a spot toward the end and ordered some buffalo wings and a beer. He'd just tipped up the beer when a familiar face leaned into his range of vision.

Roger Ashforth.

Jack turned his head for a clearer look. Yep, that was him, the stuff-shirted, arrogant twerp. Jack took a long drink, chasing away the hot summer night's thirst. The beer didn't slake his guilt, though, or the nagging fear Marcy wouldn't get over her anger and disappointment, no matter what he said or did.

The group next to Jack left, leaving an empty space between him and Roger. Jack glanced over again. The man didn't look so sophisticated right now. The tie was gone, and so was the jacket. A stream of ketchup dribbled down the front of his pleated, tailored shirt, and he still wore the cummerbund. He looked ridiculous and half drunk.

He was sober enough to recognize Jack, though. "Well, if it isn't the maid of honor," Roger called out. "Did she kick you out, too?"

"I just wanted something to eat," Jack answered. *Lame, buddy. You can do better than that.* "She had a headache, so I left so she could get some rest. No surprise, considering the circumstances."

Roger slid off his stool and stalked toward Jack. As he moved closer, Jack noticed he had a spot of mustard next to the ketchup. "You have an odd way of interpreting events," he said.

"I call it as I see it. Don't be a sore loser."

"Oh? Why not?" He swung at Jack, clipping him on the chin.

Jack slipped sideways off the stool and grabbed at the bar. "What the hell do you think you're doing? Are you nuts or just drunk?"

"Not yet." Roger grabbed Jack's beer and tipped it to his lips.


Marcy had never heard anything so awful. Loud and off-key, with an irregular rhythm, two voices bellowed out a bawdy song outside her door. She'd heard tomcats sing better. When they began to knock on her door in time, sort of, with the tune, she buried her head under a pillow. Just what she needed, drunken party animals who couldn't find the right apartment.

"Marcy!" More pounding followed the shout.

"Jack?" she whispered in the dark.

"Marcy, we need to talk to you."

"Roger?"

She rolled out of bed and grabbed a robe. "Can my life get any worse?" she muttered on the way to the front door.

A look through the peephole revealed Jack and Roger, arm in arm. Roger's shirt hung open, and he had the cummerbund to his tux slung over one shoulder. Jack wore a hat with a duck bill for a brim.

Blowing out a frustrated breath, she unlocked the door and opened it. "Will you two shut up before you get me evicted?"

"We've reached an agreement," Roger announced.

"I've awakened in an alternate dimension," she muttered. They stood before her, arms flung across each other's shoulders, looking like best buddies coming home from a night on the town.

"We're trading places," Jack said.

"Yep. Jack's going to marry you, and I'll be the best man . . . bridesmaid . . . whatever. Heck, I'll be both," Roger said, swaying against the doorframe.

"You decided this while staring through the bottom of a beer bottle," she surmised.

"No, we flipped a coin," Jack slurred. "It's a good system. Worked for everything we had to decide tonight."

Marcy took a step backward and slammed the door in their faces.

"Oops!" she heard Jack say.

"Come on, let us in," Roger called. "We're sorry."

"Really sorry," Jack called out, then launched into a really awful rendition of "Who's Sorry Now." Roger joined in, a stanza late, as though he'd decided to sing in rounds, just like summer camp.

"Damn it, anyway." She opened the door and caught Jack's sleeve, tugging him in. Roger followed, still singing.

"Hush, you're making my head pound," she admonished. She led the way into the living room and pushed them both toward the couch. "Hand over the car keys, and then sit," she ordered, one hand outstretched to each of them.

With a sheepish look, Roger produced his. Jack patted his pockets and shrugged. "Must've left them in the car. I think. Or maybe I just can't find 'em. Wanna help me look?" He winked, then took a step toward her and stubbed his foot on the coffee table.

"Aack! Damn!" He hopped on one foot, and Marcy realized he was in his sock feet.

"Where are your shoes?"

He shrugged. "Maybe with my keys."

"You're pitiful, both of you," she told them. "I'll use the kitchen phone."

She made the arrangements, then slipped into the bathroom to splash cold water on her face. As she straightened, she stared at her reflection, noting the puffiness that lingered around her eyes, evidence of the tears she'd managed to hold back until Jack left.

She felt like crying again, but not for the same reason. She wasn't angry anymore, just tired and disappointed. She'd tricked herself into thinking she'd

# THE BRIDE'S BEST MAN 161

fallen in love with one man, then found herself falling for a man who'd been there all along. Falling for someone who had to get drunk and flip a coin to even tolerate the term "marriage" in connection with the two of them.

Marcy wasn't kidding herself. Tomorrow, aside from a killer hangover, he'd have a major case of regrets—assuming he even remembered this episode.

By the time the cab arrived, the singing had stopped. Roger sat in the wing chair, humming show tunes. He'd loosened his shoelaces, then propped his feet on the coffee table in a pose so unlike the self-contained man she'd been engaged to that she kept stealing amazed glances in his direction. If she hadn't been so exasperated, she might have collapsed into giggles.

"Your ride's here," she told Roger, hoisting him from the chair and pointing him toward the door. She tried to do the same for Jack, but he'd stretched out on the sofa and fallen asleep. "Come on, wake up!" She nudged him, then caught his hand to pull him upright.

A snuffling snore was his only response. She tugged hard, but he didn't awaken. She glanced at Roger. "You could help." He started to slide down the wall he'd been leaning against.

"I don't need this," she muttered, giving up on Jack and heading for Roger. After escorting him to the cab and sending him on his way, she headed back upstairs. She could call another cab for Jack, or she could let him sleep. The latter was less trouble, plus it offered the opportunity for an explanation in the morning. She still was furious with him. Even stronger than her anger, though, was an intense curiosity. Never in her strangest dreams would she have imagined what had happened tonight. She wasn't letting Jack out of the apartment until she had the full story.

# NINE

A sound in the apartment awakened Marcy from a restless sleep. A board creaked. Then she heard a thump in the kitchen. She blinked in the darkness, staring at the bedroom door, wishing she'd closed it, wondering if she was still dreaming.

Her body felt hot and languid. Isolated images flashed through her mind, fuzzy and indistinct, fading with each passing second. She glanced at the bedside clock. Four A.M. The dark before dawn.

Maybe she wasn't really awake. Lucid dreaming, wasn't that the term for something like this? She reached out to touch the clock. Its metal casing felt cool against her fingertips.

Footsteps sounded in the hallway. A thin sliver of light appeared around the edge of her door. Fear fluttered in her throat for an instant before she remembered Jack was here. It must be him on the way to the bathroom. No doubt he'd awakened with a headache and was searching for some aspirin.

He hesitated just outside her bedroom door, and the smell of stale cigarette smoke clinging to his clothes wafted into the room. She knew he never smoked, that it was the smell of the smoke-heavy bar with the added tinge of sour, spilled whiskey and sweat.

"Jack? Are you all right?" She hoped he wasn't going to be sick.

"Sorry I woke you," he said. The sliver of light widened, and he leaned through the opening. "I just wanted to rinse the fuzzy taste out of my mouth."

She sat up, watching him for a moment. "I wasn't sleeping too well anyway." Her voice was husky from sleep, or from the sudden emotion that tightened her throat. "How are you feeling?"

"Better than I should. Are you still mad?"

"Maybe." She wasn't, not in her heart. She never could stay mad at him. Her head told her she ought not to let him off the hook too easily, though. Rampant testosterone ought not to be encouraged, as his own mother would put it.

He glanced away from her, his profile backlit by the hall light. "I guess you have a few reasons to be angry. I'll head on home now and be out of your way."

"Better not. I'm not sure you'd pass a Breathalyzer test."

He held silent for a moment, then sighed. "I have a confession to make. I only had one beer."

"Feed me another line."

"It's true." He scratched his chin, his head tilted at a sheepish angle. Marcy recognized the telling gesture. Her instincts told her not only was he was telling the truth, but he expected her to lambaste him for that stunt.

"So you faked it all."

"All but the singing." He shrugged. "I didn't want

Roger to feel bad about making such an idiot of himself, and I wanted to stick around to answer the phone in case he decided to make an even bigger idiot of himself after he got home—or changed his mind about going home."

She flung a pillow at him, hitting him squarely in the chest. "And what about me? Did you enjoy putting one over on me, waking up neighbors, and embarrassing me?"

An audible sigh filled the room, like the first breeze that precedes a building storm. "I got a little carried away," he admitted. "I was playing along, trying to keep the guy from getting hurt. He was pretty well loaded when I ran into him, and he was feeling pretty belligerent. He took a swing at me."

"Roger?"

"Yeah, well he's a different sort of guy when he's liquored up. But you know what the hippies used to say. Make love, not war. So I convinced him I'd make a better friend than an enemy."

"You slugged him?" She frowned, picturing the two of them when they returned. She couldn't remember any bruises on either of them. "It must not have been much of a fight."

"Nah. I bought him another drink. After he'd finished that one and another, we started to talk."

"I'm afraid to ask what about."

"Guy stuff. You don't want to know. Anyway, I think we made peace and he's accepted how things are with you and me."

Her heart fluttered at the husky note in his voice. "And how are things?"

"You tell me." He strode into the room, stopping by the bed.

"Why did you watch out for Roger?"

Jack sat on the edge of the mattress and reached a hand out to stroke her cheek. "You cared for him enough that you almost married him."

"But I didn't."

"I figured if something happened to him, it would hurt you. I figured if I hurt him, even under the present circumstances, you'd slug me. And I know from experience you have a mean right hook. At least you did when we were six."

His touch was gentle, loving. She released a soft sigh, remembering the dream she'd awakened from—not the images, but the lingering heat, the emotions.

"I've grown up since then, remember?"

"I wasn't taking any chances." She heard the uncertainty in his voice. "I'd cut out my own heart before I'd hurt you unnecessarily."

She pulled away from him and tucked her knees against her chest beneath the thin sheet, fighting the shivers his touch evoked. She wasn't ready yet to let him off the hook, not when this fine feeling that had been unleashed within her might be hers alone.

"You thought it necessary to break off my engagement with Roger."

He sat beside her. "I can't honestly say I'm sorry. Call me selfish, but the only regret I have is that it took me so long to realize how I really feel about you."

She stole a glance at him from beneath her lashes. "And that is?"

"You're my heart. If I were a better man, I'd have known it all along."

She stared at him in the semidarkness. "Don't move," she ordered.

"Huh?"

She leaned past him and switched on the bedside lamp, then stared at him, blinking as her eyes adjusted to the brightness. "And that kiss?" she asked after a moment. She studied his expression, searching for the truth in the serious lines fanning out from the corners of his eyes, in the straight line of his lips.

He met her gaze steadily. "The best move I ever made. And the funny thing is, I wasn't even planning it." A rueful smile curved his lips as he reached for her hands and laced his fingers between hers. "I'd changed my mind about interfering, decided I was being a selfish jerk and that I should take the high road because if you thought Roger would make you happy, then that's who you should marry."

"Then why did you kiss me that first time?"

"Couldn't help myself." He moved suddenly, kissing her hard.

He caught her by surprise. Her mouth opened in a surprised gasp, and he took full advantage, sliding his tongue inside to tease and taste. His hands cupped her face, and she felt the trembling in his fingertips. He tasted of mint, of her brand of mouthwash, and the other subtle flavor that was simply Jack.

Desire shot through her, hot and demanding. She forgot to breathe, forgot everything except the need coursing through her veins.

She kissed him back with all the pent-up need that had been building within her. She shifted, straightening her legs so she could lean toward him. She grasped his shoulders, feeling the taut, bunched muscles. He seemed to be holding himself in check, but just barely.

She could feel it in the tense coil of the muscles beneath her fingertips, in the demanding, almost desperate way he kissed her. Her breasts tightened in response, and she leaned closer, feeling the brush of her nipples against Jack's chest. Her thin nightshirt might as well not have been there, so sensitive had her breasts become to the sensations, to the heat of his flesh beneath the thin fabric that kept skin from touching skin.

She shifted again, restless, wanting more. His hands traced a path of fire down her neck, shoulders, and spine, and finally cupped her hips. Sensations she'd barely imagined tingled along her nerve endings.

He sat back, and Marcy moaned deep in her throat, not wanting him to pull away. He kissed her quickly, then moved to the sensitive place beneath her earlobe. The feel of it turned her bones to mush. She shivered as he kissed his way slowly down her neck to the base of her throat. Tipping her head back to give him access, she moaned.

It was the same as that day at the lake, except this time they had no audience, no slippery lake bottom, no water up to the waist. It was just the two of them, here alone, and they had a bed.

"You like this?" he asked softly.

"What do you think?" She pulled open his shirt, wanting to touch more of him. He must have felt the same, because he reached beneath the tail of her nightshirt, and with one swift motion he pulled it over her head and tossed it to the floor.

He leaned back for a moment, studying her, his eyes glazed with a passion that mirrored her own. Her skin burned where his gaze touched her. "Perfect," he whispered, reaching out. "I haven't seen you like this since we were about four years old. You've changed some."

A sultry laugh bubbled up from deep within her. "I wasn't that precocious."

He grinned. "No, just this naked." He reached out, letting his fingers trace the path his eyes had followed an instant before.

"As I recall, we both were more naked than this." She gasped as his hands brushed across the tips of her nipples. Heat shot through her and pooled between her thighs, moist and wanting.

"Buck naked, dancing under the summer sun with the garden sprinkler going full blast." He fluttered his fingers across her skin, mimicking the fall of water droplets. It didn't feel like water, but Marcy recognized the memories in his movements. The memories were a link, a bond that should have distracted her from the passion of the moment. Instead, they only stoked her desire.

*Cradle to grave.*

She knew at that moment she'd loved him all her life and would love him with her last breath. Through the years, that love had changed. Maybe it would change again. She couldn't predict the future, didn't even want to consider it. Only the present mattered. Doing it right. Making the most of the moment.

The most.

His fingers were driving her insane, creating a firestorm. She wondered if she could affect him as intensely. She reached for his shirt and peeled it off his shoulders. "I think you still have too many clothes on."

And when she'd dispensed with the shirt, her fingers plucked at his belt buckle. His sharp intake of breath thrilled her. She slowly unbuckled his belt, then teased it from the loops.

She felt him stiffen. Then he moved like lightning, tugging her against him, his body pressed intimately against hers. He kissed her, long and intense. He was breathing hard when he allowed a fraction of an inch between their lips.

"Are you sure you know what you're doing?"

"Exactly."

"I'll leave if you ask me to."

"Don't you dare," she whispered. She wriggled against him, impatient now that she could feel the hard bulge in his jeans pressing against her. She reached between them, unsnapped his jeans, and slid down the zipper. Then she teased him with her fingertips.

With one swift, fluid motion, he rolled her beneath him and kissed her until she couldn't even think. Then he pushed off the bed, shed his jeans, and returned to her.

Raw need overtook conscious thought. "Now," she whispered.

He didn't protest, just inched her panties downward, kissing the path of the fabric over her skin. She kicked them off when they reached her ankles, and he kissed the return path.

When his tongue touched the sensitive spot between her legs, she nearly exploded. "Now," she insisted. "Now." She sat up, then scooted toward him and wrapped her legs around his waist. With a gentle touch, he slipped a finger inside her, testing her readiness. And he nearly took her over the edge.

Shifting slightly, he gripped her hips. She stared into his eyes, breathing his breath, feeling his raw need as strong as her own. Then he slid inside her.

Her body pulsed around him, and then he was moving, stroke after stroke, in an intense rhythm of pleasure and raw, hot need. Pleasure so intense it brought tears to her eyes. She tipped her head back, shuddering as they found their release in the same instant. She clutched at him, wrapping her arms around him, holding him tightly until the pleasure peaked, then eased to satiation.

Her body felt limp and boneless, and still she didn't move, just relaxed her hold and rested her head on his shoulder. "Amazing. Who'd have thought?"

His deep, satisfied sigh fanned the heated flesh along the nape of her neck. "All that time wasted when we could have been doing this together."

She smiled against him. "Maybe we just weren't ready for each other yet."

"Hmm. Maybe. Thirsty?"

"Parched. I'll get us some tea." Reluctantly she pulled away and slid off the bed. She was reaching for her robe when he grabbed her from behind and pulled her back onto the bed. "What?" she said, giggling as he rolled her beneath him.

"One thing," he said.

"Yes?" She licked her lips, an unplanned gesture of anticipation. She did it without thinking. When she realized it, she hesitated, then repeated the motion.

"Next time, do you want it hot and fast, or slow and drawn out until you scream and beg me to take you?"

"Oh, aren't you full of yourself," she retorted, giggling. She shoved him off her and wriggled away. Dodging his grasping hands, she headed toward the kitchen.

He caught up with her in the hallway and dropped a kiss on the nape of her neck. "Forgot your robe." He stepped back and held it out, helping her into it. Then he cinched the waist and adjusted the neck. "Don't flash anybody out in the parking lot," he said. "I don't want to share."

She poked him in the solar plexus. "Me either, Nature Boy." She backed a few steps away and subjected him to a thorough, appreciative, head-to-toe examination. Strong shoulders, well-honed by his work during the week and his weekends outdoors. Trim waist, firm abdomen, with a light dusting of dusky brown hair that arrowed lower. His desire, already returning so obviously.

"Wanna help?"

"I've never made love in a kitchen before."

She smirked. "Who would've thought? Wait for me in the bedroom, Nature Boy."

He watched her until she turned the corner toward

# THE BRIDE'S BEST MAN

the kitchen, she knew. Then the floorboard outside her bedroom squeaked. The stereo on the dresser came on. The board at the foot of the bed sounded next.

Marcy smiled in the darkness and shook her head. Who would've thought it? She and Jack. And who would've thought it would be so amazing, that they'd fit so well together? She opened the refrigerator and stood there for a moment, fanning herself. The chilled air cooled her heated skin, but it had little effect on the heat already rising inside her.

She fixed their drinks, then grabbed some cheese and crackers. She remembered him telling her once that sex always made him hungry.

Balancing it all on a small tray, she started back down the hall. "Turn off the hall light," he told her when she reached the doorway. He stood across the room, backlit this time by the pale light from the window. Behind him, she could see the full moon rising over the next building. He still wore nothing but a smile.

He'd lit every candle in her room, three on the dresser, two on the chest, and three each on the bedside tables. He glanced at the tray. "A woman who'll let me eat crackers in bed, too. I've died and gone to heaven."

She set the tray on the nearest nightstand. "Just don't dribble crumbs in the sheets."

"I never dribble, at least since I was three."

"Five," she retorted. "I distinctly remember your dribbling in kindergarten. And then there's that redhead you went out with last year."

"No, darlin', that was drooling. And it was only because I was still practicing." He took a step closer, and Marcy felt her breath catch at his expression.

"All that practice must have done some good," she teased. "I should send thank-you notes." With the moonlight at his back, the candlelight flickering beside him, he was all hard planes and shadows. She was finding it difficult to keep up the familiar banter. She ought to feel awkward at this change in their relationship. Maybe she would in the morning. Right now, she simply concentrated on breathing.

And feeling.

He cupped her cheeks and kissed her, slow and sweet. And she melted against him.

They made love again. This time it wasn't raw, but exquisitely tender. They took their time, learning the feel of each other, learning each freckle and dimple by candlelight. She savored each touch, each kiss, giving, taking, and loving. She thought she'd loved before, but those experiences were only pale imitations compared to this night.

And when they were done, she curled against him, spoon fashion. He held her tightly and nuzzled her neck.

"I could stay like this forever," he whispered.

"We'd both go bankrupt." One of the candles on the nightstand fluttered. "We'd better blow those out."

She rolled away from him and stood. One by one, she blew out the flames. When she finished, she slipped back into his arms. For a long time, she lay there, listening to him breathe.

Finally, she drifted into a deep, exhausted sleep.

# THE BRIDE'S BEST MAN

\* \* \*

A shaft of sunlight cut through the gap in the drapes, disturbing Marcy's sleep. She shifted slightly, snuggling closer to Jack as she sought to return to the peaceful oblivion she'd fallen into sometime in the wee hours before dawn. The morning light proved too stubborn, though. It spread across the bed, throwing a golden glow across the rumpled sheets.

Marcy stretched and glanced around, smiling when she became aware of Jack's hand splayed intimately across her breast. Then his soft snore sounded in her ear.

She'd forgotten he snored.

His wasn't the startling rumble she recalled from childhood visits to her grandfather's farm. Grandpa's snores were the freight train variety. Jack's reminded her more of the gentle rumble of distant thunder—comforting under the right circumstances, but with the potential to wreak havoc on those in its path. At the moment, Jack's soft snore had more in common with an approaching storm than she wanted to consider.

She started to rise, but his arm tightened across her chest, pulling her closer. "Morning?" he mumbled close to her ear. The sensation sent delicious shivers down her spine. Fingers of unease threaded through the desire his closeness evoked, keeping her still in his arms.

"It's still early," she whispered. Last night it all had seemed so clear to her—take what she wanted, enjoy the moment for what it was and for as long as it lasted.

It had been easier in the golden glow of the flickering candlelight. Time out of mind, a time apart.

And now that time was past, and the sharp light of the morning after cut between the gap in the drawn curtains. She felt unsettled, uncertain how to proceed, uncertain what this new twist in their friendship meant. Fear, too, lay beneath her uneasiness, the fear that they'd made a huge mistake and thrown a lifelong friendship in the sewer for the sake of one night's passion.

Carefully, she eased herself out of Jack's embrace and rose from the bed. He stirred briefly, then rolled to his side and wrapped his arms around her pillow. He inhaled deeply, as if savoring the lingering scent of her perfume on the pillowcase. Her heart skipped a beat, and she almost crawled back into bed with him.

She didn't, though. She couldn't. She needed to think, and she couldn't do that with him curled against her in this bed. Stealthily, she gathered up a fresh set of clothes and her running shoes and slipped from the room to dress. Then she let herself out of the apartment, hurried out the main entrance, and settled into an easy jogging pace as she made her way along the quiet sidewalks toward the park.

Down to the end of the block and around the corner. *What was I thinking, taking Jack into my bed after the stunt he pulled with Roger last night?*

Half a block, cross the street during a break in traffic, cut through the hedge bordering the park. *Sleeping with my best friend. No, not sleeping . . . there was very little sleeping going on in that bed.*

She couldn't help the silly smile that stole onto her

lips as she remembered exactly what had been going on. *Admit it, girl, he made you feel boneless, like you'd died and gone to heaven. Who cares whether he woke up the entire block? Whether he tricked you into letting him stay? He did it for all the right reasons, or you'd never have let him into your bed.*

She stumbled on a root, then righted herself and found her stride again. Across the paved parking lot, past the swings, and onto the jogging trail that meandered between the trees. Jack, her friend. Jack, her newfound lover. Jack who'd made her feel like the queen of the world, like something precious to be admired and stroked. Treasured and pleasured. Jack, who'd been her best friend for as long as she could remember, the one man she could trust never to hurt her.

*At least he wouldn't mean to hurt me.*

Just the thought triggered a painful twinge in her heart. She picked up her pace and turned onto the path that circled the large pond at the center of the park. Twice around, then back onto the woodland trail, through the trees toward the soccer fields. Gradually, the rhythmic motion eased the worst of her fears.

It was done. They'd made love, and she couldn't turn back the clock, even if she wanted to. The more she tumbled the memories through her mind, the more certain she became that last night had been inevitable. Every moment since he'd kissed her at the Rose Festival had led in that direction. Every touch, every glance, every subsequent kiss—exquisite foreplay in every moment they'd spent together.

So now what?

She dodged a stray ball from an early soccer practice as she circled the back of the field, then picked up her pace, forcing her feet into a faster rhythm.

*Now what? Now what? Now what?*

The question beat through her brain with the insistent rhythm of her running steps. No answers came—images, dreams, wishes, but no answers. She could picture the two of them together as they'd always been, laughing, teasing, and having fun with the added bonus of long, wickedly pleasurable nights together. Those images alone added heat to her body, which already was sweating profusely from exertion.

Another image popped unbidden to her mind. The wedding dress Jack had helped her choose, her at the altar with him beside her. She rejected the image immediately. Jack wasn't marriage material. She knew that better than anyone. She knew *him* better than anyone, and she wasn't fool enough to think she could convince him to alter the foundation of his entire system of beliefs at this late date.

She'd simply take things as they came, day by day, and live for once on his terms—enjoy the present and not try to make more of the relationship. She could do that. She really could. To do otherwise was to court certain heartbreak.

As the thought settled into acceptance, she turned her footsteps back toward the apartment. Sweat beaded on her forehead and soaked a wet vee down the front of her shirt. She needed nothing more than a long, refreshing shower. Maybe, she thought with a glimmer of anticipation, Jack would join her and work more of his magic on her.

Live for the moment, that would be her creed. And oh, what moments there could be.

The excitement built within her as she neared her building. She picked up her pace and raced up the steps and through the lobby to the stairs. By the time she reached her floor, she couldn't hold back a wide grin.

The door was unlocked, just as she'd left it. She kicked off her shoes and started to tiptoe into the hallway. Then the image of him joining her in the shower flickered through her mind. She halted, realizing it wasn't going to happen if he slept through the event.

Backtracking, she opened the door and gave it a good slam. Then she clomped as loudly as she could manage with her bare feet. "Hey, sleepyhead," she called as she reached the bedroom.

Nothing but silence greeted her—no whispered hello, no groan of dismay at being awakened, not even a rustling of the sheets or a creak of the floor. She peered inside and gasped with dismay. The carefully made bed bore no signs of last night's lovemaking. His clothes were gone, and hers were neatly folded on the corner chair. Only the candles remained as a reminder of the night before, clustered in groups of three and four on the nightstands and the dresser.

The bathroom mirror still bore the mist from Jack's shower, and he'd draped the damp towel over the rack. She touched it, wishing fervently that she hadn't gone for a run, that she'd stayed here in the apartment and shared that shower with him. Instead, she'd run away, literally, although only to sort out her thoughts and feelings.

No, she'd run away because she was a coward, because she didn't want to risk seeing regret in his eyes as he awakened.

She wondered if he'd been relieved to find her gone when he awakened. Maybe, just maybe, he'd been hurt that she'd left without a word. She hadn't even left him a note telling him where she'd gone.

"Gawd, Marcy, you're such an idiot," she muttered, immediately jumping from her chair to reach for the phone. She snatched up the receiver and dialed his number. When the answering machine clicked on, she hesitated, then hung up. She simply didn't know what to say. "Thanks for the good time" seemed too crass. Yet an admission of how much she regretted not finding him here on her return might make him twist the knife of guilt he could be feeling over last night's events.

And if he'd been disappointed to find her gone? Hmm. How did one discern this? Was there an appropriately generic message for the morning after that covered all the bases? The situation certainly was outside her experience—and there was too much at stake to get it wrong.

Or was there? What were the chances Jack was agonizing over questions like this? What were the chances any man would?

"Marcy, you're a really big idiot," she repeated. She'd just resolved to take things one day at a time and live for the moment, and here she was obsessing over what she might have done or should have done.

"Marcy, just take a shower and get on with the day," she told herself.

Feeling every bit as jittery as she had when she'd left the apartment earlier, she stripped off her sweaty clothes and turned on the shower. Moments later, she was beneath the spray, washing away the sweat from her run. The sweet apple scent of her favorite soap filled her nostrils and eased some of her displeasure. She tipped her head back and closed her eyes, forcing the thought of everything except the moment from her mind. Live for the moment. Live for the moment.

The scent of hot cappuccino drifted around her, mingling with the soapy apple fragrance. Her stomach growled in response. "What the—"

The shower door slid open suddenly, startling a gasp from her. Jack stood in the opening, a wide, appreciative grin spreading across his face as he let his gaze drift lazily down her body, then back to her eyes. "Hungry?" he asked at last.

# TEN

Marcy stared at Jack, tongue-tied. Relief flooded through her, followed quickly by an awareness of her nakedness. She almost reached for the towel, but realized how ridiculous that would look considering how much of her he'd seen and touched and kissed last night.

"You brought cappuccino?" she said, reaching for the shampoo instead.

He nodded. "Plus croissants, cream puffs, and jelly doughnuts. I think I need to wash my hands before eating, though." He kicked off his shoes and stepped into the shower with her, still fully dressed.

"Most people would just use the sink," she replied, laughing.

He kissed her hard and quick, then reached for the soap. "Most people don't have you wet, naked, and slippery in the shower with them. A good thing, too, because they'd never want to get out, and then the city would run out of water, leaving the populace high, dry, and prune-fingered."

"You're ridiculous. And you're very wet."

"Terrible, isn't it? And I don't have anything dry to put on. You know what that means, don't you?"

She grinned and turned to face the shower spray. "Wash my back," she ordered.

He did, moving with slow, tantalizing strokes. Then he washed her legs, her neck, and her breasts. At last, his fingers dipped lower into the hot, moist place where her desire pooled. Her knees buckled as he slipped one finger inside, teasing that tiny, most sensitive point until she groaned with pleasure.

Wave after wave of pure ecstasy shook her body as she leaned back against the shower wall for support. The spray from the showerhead felt cool compared with the heat building inside her.

Suddenly, icy water shot from the shower, shocking a shriek from her. Jack jerked in surprise, then groaned. "You need a bigger hot water heater."

She switched off the water quickly, then grabbed his shirtfront and yanked him toward her as she released a low, catlike growl. "What I need is you."

His eyes widened at her boldness, but his twinkle of appreciation mingling with surprise spurred her on. She kissed him slowly, with every ounce of seduction she could muster. Then she took his hand and led him back to the bedroom.

His shirt landed with a plop on the hallway floor. His pants landed next to the bed. She pulled his dripping socks off and tossed them aside, not caring where they landed. "I'm so glad you came back," she admitted.

"Me, too," he answered, but not until after another of those toe-curling kisses. And then, for a while, there was no time or breath to be wasted on talking.

Later, Marcy lay half asleep in Jack's arms, savoring

the lingering sensations from their lovemaking. Her thoughts drifted back to the moment only an hour or so before when she'd realized she'd returned to an empty apartment. Just the memory made her throat tighten with anxiety.

She must have made some sound, or perhaps Jack felt the stiffening in her spine as she struggled to force the feeling back.

"What are you thinking?" he asked, his fingers absently stroking her back. The sensation was more soothing than sensual, and Marcy closed her eyes to savor it.

"Nothing much," she whispered. "Just wishing we could stay like this forever."

"Who's to say we can't?"

She felt him shift, and her eyelids fluttered open. Here in the half-light of her bedroom, his expression relaxed and tender, a thin sheen of sweat covering his body, he seemed so different than the man she'd thought she knew. Serious as well as playful. Considerate in ways she hadn't imagined. Strong, muscular, hard where he should be, yet with smooth, so very touchable skin. So many details she'd noticed in passing but never truly appreciated until now. No wonder she'd always felt something was missing in her relationships with other men. They'd had the right résumé, but not the right heart, the right laugh. None of them had been Jack.

At that moment, she understood what had eluded her all these years.

She loved Jack. Completely. With every cell of her body, every pulsing beat of her heart. He wasn't just her friend and her lover. He was her one true love.

The realization sent a twisted tangle of emotions through her, stealing her breath. Intense joy mingled with equally intense sorrow, because loving Jack was an uncertain and rocky path. It didn't fit her dreams for the future. He didn't share her dreams. Ultimately, she knew, she'd have to give up one or the other, Jack or the dreams. Worse yet, she might lose both.

He must have sensed the change in her, the unsettled nature of her thoughts. He shifted so he could see her face. "Something's bothering you."

She sighed, wondering how much to tell him, knowing if she said too much she might drive him away too soon. He was too astute, too aware of her moods, though, to believe she wasn't troubled.

"When I came back and found you gone," she began, then bit her lip, hesitating.

"I heard you go out for your morning run and figured you'd be hungry when you got back. I'd planned to be back sooner, but the corner shop was out of jelly doughnuts, so I had to go over to the one on Main."

"I thought you just wanted to get away from me, that maybe you were sorry about last night. I know better now, but right then I thought we'd made a big mistake and screwed up everything—the friendship, everything."

"I should have left a note," he whispered. He propped himself on one elbow and stroked her cheek, his expression tender. "I can't say I've never been in a rush to get away in the morning light, or even long before then. That was different. I wasn't with you. It's so different with you, so perfect because with you there's trust and caring and a shared past that means more than I can put into words."

Marcy's throat tightened at his admission. She nodded. "That's why I was afraid," she managed.

He pulled her against him, holding her tightly. They lay that way for a while, needing no more words. At least that's what Marcy thought.

"Marry me," he whispered in her ear.

She stiffened, sure she must have heard him wrong. "What did you say?"

"Marry me." He rolled her beneath him and propped himself on his elbows above her, his face inches from her. "I want us to get married. Heck, you already have the dress. Believe me, I've dreamed about you in that dress and—"

"Have you lost your mind?" she asked.

"Maybe. More likely I finally came to my senses."

She stared up at him, her eyes wide with amazement, her heart pounding so loudly she could barely hear her own thoughts. "Morning-after guilt," she muttered.

"No way."

"I know you too well."

"Then you know I have never in my life proposed to a woman out of guilt—in fact, I've never proposed before. And much as it pains me to admit it at this moment, I happen to be more of an expert on morning-after guilt than you—unless you've been holding back a lot of secrets all these years."

She pushed against his chest, shoving him off her so she could sit upright. She thought better with her fingers at her temples, her arms propped on her knees and the sheet pulled over her chest so she didn't feel so naked—so exposed. "OK, I'll concede that point. But you don't want to marry me."

"I do."

She shook her head. "You're saying that because you know that's what I've always wanted—getting married, that is—and because you helped screw up my engagement. You're just being a good friend."

He leaned against her, wrapping his arms around her, clasping his hands above hers at her knees. "What can I say to convince you?"

"You can't," she answered, feeling a bittersweet longing for what she knew they couldn't have. "I know you too well to believe that's what you truly want. It's very sweet of you to suggest it, though. Only my best friend would even consider such a sacrifice."

"Hmmph," was his only answer. He squeezed her against him, then released a long sigh that must have come the depths of his soul. Relief, perhaps, or a misplaced sense of guilt still hammering away at him. Then Marcy's stomach growled loudly, interrupting the awkward silence that had fallen between them.

"Maybe we should feed that thing before it goes hunting on its own." Jack rolled away from her and stood beside the bed.

Marcy grinned as she forcefully put the bittersweet moment behind her. "Not a bad idea, Nature Boy. Are we dressing for breakfast or dining in the buff?" She winked as her gaze traveled down his body, enjoying the sight of his lean muscles, the springy curls of chest hair, his taut abdomen, and the stiffening evidence of his response to her blatant perusal.

Jack jerked the sheet from the bed and wrapped it around his waist. "I'm feeling suddenly shy. Besides, Mrs. Robertson hasn't been over yet with her usual Sunday invitation to tea."

"Good point." Marcy grabbed her robe and cinched the tie at the waist. She was halfway into the hallway when she started to giggle. "Maybe we should get dressed. If we went to the door like this, we'd probably shock her into a heart attack."

"You can if you want to, but I don't have anything to put on." He picked up the still sodden shirt from the hallway floor, then let it fall. It made a splatting sound that triggered another giggle from Marcy.

"You know where the dryer is, and you know how to use it," she said, then spun on her heel. "I'll be too busy snarfing down doughnuts and cold cappuccino."

His sigh followed her as she headed toward the kitchen. "This is a bitter omen," he called after her.

"Nice try. Take care of your laundry, Nature Boy." She grinned as she spotted two doughnut bags on the counter beside two extra large Styrofoam cups from the corner shop. As she set out plates and poured the cappuccino into mugs to warm in the microwave, she heard him open the door to the utility closet and toss his clothes into the dryer. A moment later, he joined her, still wearing the floral print sheet from her bed.

"You look good in roses," she quipped.

He winked. "It's our flower." His lips curved into a teasing smile, but his stare contained a serious, almost vulnerable note. Emotion darkened his eyes as the smile faded. He seemed to be waiting for something.

She sat very still, then caught his hand and kissed

it. "I suppose they are." The Rose Festival. The painting he'd bought her. The wild briars by their fishing spot at the creek.

The microwave dinged, cutting through the silence. He squeezed her hand, then released it to retrieve the mugs. "Let's eat before we both faint from starvation," he said, sounding more like his usual self. Only the faint roughness in his tone remained of the vulnerable side he'd briefly revealed.

As Marcy selected a rich, cream-filled éclair and took a careful bite, she watched him from beneath her lashes. Could it be, she wondered, that he'd been as deeply affected as she had? Hope flared briefly within her, the emotion swelling with a life of its own. Her mind, however, quashed it before it could reach full bloom.

It was just as she'd told him. She knew him too well. No matter how much he cared for her, how much their lovemaking meant to him, the outcome would be the same. Jack was simply Jack. She had to accept him as he was without trying to change him, without expecting more than he was capable of giving.

"What are your plans for the day?" she asked, as much to distract herself from her troubling thoughts as out of any real curiosity.

He glanced at the clock on the wall. "One o'clock. A little late to go fishing, I'd say." He took another big bite of a doughnut, wiped dripping purple jelly from his chin, and chewed thoughtfully.

"I have some work to catch up on at the office," Marcy said. "I suppose I ought to go in, but I don't feel like it."

He shook his head. "Nope, I have a much better idea."

"What's that?"

He grinned as he lifted another doughnut. "It's a surprise. I just need to make a quick phone call while you take a shower."

Her eyebrows arched in a challenge. "I already had a shower."

He leaned across the table to place a kiss on the tip of her nose. "You smell like sex, and while I think it's a very, very nice, seductive, wonderfully terrific perfume, you might be a bit self-conscious about it once you realize where we're going."

She could feel a flush rising from the tips of her toes to suffuse her entire body. "And that is?"

He sat back and took a big bite. He chewed for a moment, then shook his head in silence. No amount of pleading or teasing on her part could pry the answer from him.

"What should I put on after this shower?" she finally demanded.

He considered for a moment, lifting his mug and sipping thoughtfully. "Jeans," he said at last. "Good walking shoes. One of those plaid shirts of yours, and maybe a swimsuit underneath."

"Sounds like fishing clothes to me."

"Not exactly. I didn't specify the old, ratty stuff that you don't care whether you get fish slime on."

"Good point. So where are we going?"

He just grinned and shoved back his chair. "I think I'll check the dryer."

An hour later, Marcy was no closer to knowing Jack's plan for the rest of the day. He'd tossed her

# THE BRIDE'S BEST MAN 191

clean clothes into the bathroom while she showered, made a phone call, then put on his own still damp ones for the drive to his apartment. He changed clothes, made another call, then hurried her back to the car.

They stopped at a job site near the edge of the city, where he conferred briefly with the owner, inspected a damaged section of newly installed cabinetry, and made a third call.

"Why don't you just get a cell phone?" she asked him when he returned from borrowing the owner's office.

"Don't need one." He looped her arm through his and headed toward the exit.

"Who did you call this time?"

"Just somebody who knows somebody. Nothing you need to be concerned about. You'll find out soon enough."

She pulled her arm from his and stalked ahead of him toward the car. "I hate it when you get like this. You always did enjoy playing 'I've got a secret.' Well, you can just keep your secret." She held back a smile, determined to give him a taste of his own tactics.

He punched the remote to unlock the car. "OK. You want me to take you home?"

"Sure." She climbed inside and stared out the windshield. It wasn't what she wanted, but he didn't have to know that just yet. He'd been prancing around for two hours now, taunting her. She didn't mind paying him back just a little bit.

He hesitated. "Really?"

She shrugged. "Whatever."

He circled the car and climbed in behind the

wheel. He inserted the key, but didn't switch on the engine yet. "You really don't want to know what I have planned? After all the trouble I went to just to set this up?"

"Maybe you should have just asked me instead of assuming you knew what's best." She hadn't meant it as a dig, but the moment the words left her mouth she realized how it must sound. His expression sobered, then he slapped the heel of his hand against the dashboard.

"I did it again, didn't I?" He looked troubled, and she nearly confessed she'd just been teasing him, paying him back for stringing her along. Only the fact there was more than a grain of truth in her spur-of-the-moment comeback kept her silent.

"I'm sorry," he said. "I didn't think about how it might feel to you, considering the high-handed way I acted over your engagement. I didn't mean to be manipulative."

She sighed, knowing she had to let him off the hook. "I didn't think you were being manipulative. I just wanted to tease you a little. And I tripped over my tongue."

He studied her, his expression uncertain. "Then you don't want me to take you home?"

She waved a dismissive hand. "Of course not. I was just yanking your chain. A little quid pro quo. Now, if you don't mind starting the car so we can get some air-conditioning going—we're parked in the sun, and I'm melting here."

She was melting all right, into a puddle of mush just from the flash of warmth in his gaze—warmth mixed with desire and a genuine sense of apprecia-

# THE BRIDE'S BEST MAN

tion. It was a potent combination, one she wasn't accustomed to seeing reflected back at her in Jack's gaze.

He complied, switching the air on full blast. "It'll take a minute," he said, stating the obvious as hot air gushed from the vents. Marcy rolled down her window in response while he concentrated on maneuvering the car between potholes and onto the highway. "Want to know where we're going?" he asked when they were once again on their way.

She leaned back against the headrest and closed her eyes. "Nope. I love surprises." By now, the air-conditioning was beginning to have an effect, so she touched the switch to close her window.

"Women," Jack muttered in a disgusted tone. Marcy just grinned as she stole a peek at his profile. He wasn't nearly as perturbed as he'd sounded, not if the smile crinkling the crow's-feet at the corners of his eyes was any indication.

After about ten miles, he turned the car onto a side road. A mile later, they left the pavement for the gravel surface of a narrow lane that ran parallel to a small creek. The road twisted and turned, following the creek between the hills and into a valley.

At last, he turned into an narrow driveway next to a "for sale" sign bearing the emblem of a real-estate agency that referred a lot of business to Jack's company. He stopped in front of the weathered, two-story farmhouse and waved to the elderly woman who rocked on the porch swing.

"This is Sally Rose's mother, Martha Junkets," Jack explained. "Sally Rose brought me out here one time when they needed help loading some furniture Sally

Rose was taking to her daughter's place—Jackie, not Sarah. Jackie's the one who got married last year. Sarah's still in college, although Sally Rose is afraid she's going to drop out to marry the guy she's been dating. He's not a bad guy, just needs to grow up a little." His tone was that of an indulgent uncle, and he frowned a little, as if troubled by the choice he expected young Sarah to make—young Sarah, who really wasn't that much younger than the two of them.

A smile teased at Marcy's lips. Trust Jack to become involved with the entire clan and end up playing big brother to the youngest of them. "I'm sure she'll make the right choice," Marcy said.

"And that is?"

"Not for either of us to decide," she answered. "Besides, I haven't met any of them, so what do I know?"

He chuckled. "Probably more than I do. After all, I'm just a man, as Sally Rose often reminds me. Sometimes I wonder why I don't fire the woman for insubordination."

Mrs. Junkets must have heard the last, because she grinned broadly at their approach. "You don't fire her because she's the only thing between you and total chaos." She patted a large, covered basket beside her on the wide seat of the swing and laughed. "Poor boy can't even arrange a picnic by himself. You must be Marcy," the woman continued as she eased herself off the seat and held out a hand. "I'm Martha, and it's about time he brought you around here."

Confused, and equally delighted with the spunky

old woman who stood before her, Marcy simply took the hand that was offered, taking care not to put too much pressure on the swollen, misshapen joints. "Arthritis," Martha said, turning stiffly to lift the basket. "Makes it hard to keep up with things around here. That's why I put the place up for sale."

"That must have been a difficult decision."

Martha nodded, and in the faded blue of her watery eyes, Marcy caught a glimpse of sadness. "It was," Martha conceded. "Time moves on, though, and it's time some young family moved in and filled the place with children. It's too lonely out here by myself now."

Jack leaned down and kissed Martha's papery cheek. "Thanks for fixing the picnic. Is there anything you'd like me to take care of before we head down to the pond?"

Martha shook her head. "Run along now, the two of you, so I can get on with my afternoon nap. Sally Rose is coming by later to take me to evening church services, so if I'm not here when you get ready to leave, you can just set the basket on the porch."

Marcy added her thanks to Jack's, then waited as Jack lifted the picnic basket. He held the front door open for Martha, then led the way around the side of the house, through a rose arbor laden with the most fragrant deep red roses she'd ever encountered. "My mother would give her right arm for a cutting from these roses," she said, pausing for a deep sniff of the heavenly scent.

"Hmm. I might be able to arrange something," he said. "After all, I have a vested interest in keeping Cecilia happy. Can't have my future mother-in-law on my bad side—or is it the other way around?" His tone, rich with suppressed laughter, reassured her. He was just teasing her, not tumbling down the serious path he'd pursued earlier back at her apartment.

She let herself laugh with him, feeling more comfortable with this mood of his. This was the Jack she knew and understood, the one who poked fun at life and at the conventions the rest of the world took for granted. Cynical and mocking, but without the harsh edges that would have made him unpleasant instead of the charming rogue she'd come to know and love.

The path led past a small, well-tended vegetable garden and a weedy patch that must have been part of a much larger garden at one time. Then they strolled through a section of trees, past an opened gate, and into a grassy field. Marcy paused for a moment, staring down the gentle slope at the large pond nestled at the base of the hill. Large pond, small lake—it could be called either, she decided.

At the center of the lake, a thick-trunked willow presided over a small island. The only access appeared to be the rowboat tethered to the small dock at the end of the path they were following.

"What do you think?" Jack asked, following the direction of her gaze.

"It's beautiful. She must hate to sell this place."

"I thought so, too, but Sally Rose says she's tried to talk Martha out of selling, with no luck."

"Where will she go?"

"Sally Rose's place. There's plenty of room there now with both girls gone." He started down the hill, then glanced back to see if she followed. "I should have brought some poles. Sally Rose swears there's a bass in here that would put anything I've ever caught to shame."

"The granddaddy of them all, huh?"

"So she says."

He didn't stop at the base of the hill, but strode straight onto the dock and set the picnic basket into the rowboat. "It's in good shape. Martha makes sure of it 'cause Sarah and her boyfriend like to come out here to get away from the rest of the family during those big holiday gatherings."

"I could understand that," Marcy answered, picturing in her mind what one of those gatherings was likely to entail. Just Cecilia and Lizzy had been enough to send her and Jack scampering for the creek since they'd been old enough to make the trip on their own. She could imagine what it must be like with an entire house full of meddling relatives trying to tell you how to run your life.

She let Jack row out to the island after promising to handle the return trip herself. "You'll probably be fat and snoring from all the food in that basket by then," she teased.

He agreed with mock solemnity. "I wouldn't want Mrs. Martha to be insulted. Even if I have to feed some to the fish, I'll empty that basket before returning it," he vowed.

They left the rowboat at the water's edge, tying it to a small post that presumably had been installed for that purpose sometime in the distant past. After spreading the cotton sheet provided for a tablecloth, they unpacked the food—fried chicken still warm from the skillet, potato salad, and strawberry pie that smelled so fresh Marcy could have sworn the berries had been picked just that morning.

"I can't believe you had that poor old woman cook all this food for us."

He looked offended. "Do I look like some kind of Neanderthal to you?"

Her gaze narrowed suspiciously. "The evidence speaks for itself."

"I'm hurt. Truly hurt. I'll have you know I'm privy to certain information, such as the fact that Martha always makes fried chicken for Sunday dinner and several friends from church join her and each one brings a covered dish. When I talked to Sally Rose, she assured me today was no exception, and there'd be plenty of leftovers since the minister and his wife were coming as well."

Marcy glanced up from the basket, a handful of well-worn but serviceable silverware in her hand. "I'm not sure I follow that."

"Everyone brings more to eat in the interests of generosity of spirit, and then they eat less because one mustn't exhibit gluttony in the presence of a man of the cloth." He looked so serious, Marcy almost believed him.

"Really?"

He shrugged, as if he didn't quite understand it himself. "According to Sally Rose."

"So thanks to the minister, we have this lovely picnic lunch of leftovers. Or is it dinner?" She glanced at the angle of the sun and frowned. "Does it matter?"

"Not to me. I'm starved. Give me a fork."

Marcy handed it over and filled a plate for herself, knowing she'd better eat as well before her stomach growled another loud rebellion. Those doughnuts, despite their multidigit calorie count, weren't enough to compensate for all the energy she'd expended that day. And during the night. It had been nearly twenty-four hours since she'd had a substantial meal, and suddenly she was ravenous.

Even so, there was twice as much food in the basket as the two of them could eat. Once their hunger was sated and they'd each consumed a piece of pie, they packed the food away from the reach of marauding insects and leaned back on the sheet to watch puffy clouds skitter across the sky.

"There's a dragon," Marcy declared, pointing out a formation to the east.

"It's a turtle," he argued.

Laughter sputtered from her lips. "How can you say that? It's clearly a dragon. Any fool can see that."

"Must be why I think it's a turtle."

She slapped playfully at his arm, then shrieked with more laughter as he swiftly rolled her beneath him. "Say it's a turtle," he demanded, his eyes sparkling with mischief.

"Or what?"

"Or I'll have to kiss some sense into you."

Her breath fluttered in her chest, and her heart rate increased. "It's a dragon," she said, enunciating each syllable clearly.

"Silly woman." He dipped his head closer, touching his lips briefly to hers. "Now do you believe me?"

"I'm quite certain it's a dragon—scaly skin, big bumpy tail, fiery breath. It's all there." She ended in a whisper, his lips mere millimeters from hers. For a long time, neither said anything at all.

She could feel the banked passion in his touch, in his swift intake of breath as she slipped her hand beneath his shirttail, in the fast pace of his heartbeat. And within her, she felt an answering passion. Not the impatient, demanding desire of the night or this morning, but a deeper, more enduring sort, the kind that could wait until they were truly alone, until no curious eyes might spy upon them and reminisce of younger days and similar moments.

"There's something about this place," Jack said after a while, his eyes boring into hers. "It's a place that's seen a lot of life, probably a lot of love. I can feel it."

"Me, too." She supposed it was logical, knowing what she did of its history and its inhabitants. Or maybe it was simply the nostalgic image such a place evoked of simpler times and long-ago sunsets shared after a hard day's work, of the laughter of children running barefoot through the grass, cane fishing poles, and warm, fresh strawberries eaten straight from the garden.

"It must have been heaven growing up here."

"So Sally Rose says. It's still a great place to raise kids. A lot better than in the city. Probably even better than Hartford Street in Bridgeton."

She drew back, just enough for her vision to focus clearly as she studied his expression. "Probably." She wondered what he was thinking, why he'd suddenly turned so thoughtful and serious.

"We could buy this place," he said. "Raise a family. Make another generation of memories."

Tilting her head to one side, Marcy met his intent, hopeful gaze.

"This isn't what you want. Not really."

A bit of mischief crept into his smile. "I hear it has the granddaddy of all fish, just waiting for the right guy to come along and drop a hook into the water."

"Or girl," she retorted.

"We could make it a contest. Whoever catches Grandpa Bass gets breakfast in bed for a month."

"Or two," she said, refusing to take anything else he said too seriously. "It would have been nice to grow up someplace like this, although I really don't have any complaints about growing up next door to you."

"We did have some fun, didn't we?" He turned sideways and rested his head in her lap. "We could have a lot more."

"Seems to me we've had more fun in the last twenty-four hours than two grown adults have a right to."

"You think so? That it was fun?" A boyish expression of pleased surprise lit his face. For Marcy, it had the power of the sun emerging from behind a cloud. It warmed her clear through.

"Yeah," she answered softly.

"It could be more than that."

She shook her head. "Don't go there."

"I'm serious, Marcy. I've never been more serious about anything in my entire life. I just think it's going to take a little time to convince you of that."

"Hmmm. Maybe," she answered, not wanting to argue or to cloud this fine feeling that had grown between them with the hard light of reality. In time, she knew, he'd come to see what she already knew, that she didn't want him to tie himself to plans and promises just to make her happy. She didn't want to tie him at all. That, she knew, was the surest way to lose her best friend. And her heart.

# ELEVEN

Jack didn't bring up the subject of Martha's house when they got back to her apartment or during the following week on the few evenings they managed to spend together when neither had to work. He didn't mention marriage again, either.

Marcy took that as a sign she'd been right, that he'd only proposed to please her, not because it was what he wanted. She allowed herself barely a sliver of regret before pushing wishful thinking from her mind. She wasn't a fool, and she wasn't Cecilia's daughter for nothing. A confirmed optimist, Cecilia had always insisted in making the best of any situation and ignoring as much of the negative as possible. Marcy couldn't think of a better approach to her changed relationship with Jack.

Carpe diem! Seize the day. *And the night,* she amended with a secret smile that brought an odd look from the office receptionist as she delivered a stack of messages to Marcy's desk.

Halfway through the stack, she found one from Jack: *Adolpho's at seven?*

She glanced down at her conservative navy suit with its below-the-knee hemline and demurely buttoned jacket. When she'd dressed this morning, it seemed the perfect choice for her meeting with the ultraconservative CEO of Balzac Investments to go over the final bid on the computer systems his company was negotiating to buy. It wasn't right for Adolpho's, though, and it especially wasn't right for a night out on the town with Jack. He'd collapse into paroxysms of laughter at the sight of her.

Nope, she needed a little time to let her hair down, spritz and curl it a bit, and dig through the closet for something sexy enough to knock his socks off.

She glanced at the clock and grimaced. "Grace, I'm leaving early. I'd appreciate it if you'd tell anyone who calls that I'm in a meeting with a potential client. And leave a message at this number," she said, handing over the slip with Jack's message. "Tell him I'll meet him there."

The receptionist frowned. "I don't remember anything on your calendar. Did I miss—"

"You didn't miss a thing," Marcy said, reassuring the woman, who was still new enough to the job to be anxious about everything. "This just came up. If anyone asks, I'll explain tomorrow." No one would, though. The people she worked for—and with—didn't care how she spent her time as long as she got results. And she did.

She intended to get results tonight, too, but of a different kind.

Three hours later, she stood outside Adolpho's, tugging at the hem of the indecently short, clinging red dress she'd impulsively bought on the way home from the office. She took a deep breath, stepped inside, gave her name to the maître d'hôtel, and followed him to the table Jack had reserved. She was ten minutes late—deliberately—so he already was there, impatiently fiddling with the stem of his water glass. He looked right past her as she approached, then visibly started.

"Marcy?" His eyes widened in shock, then quickly warmed with appreciation. "I've never seen you quite like this. I had no idea your legs went up that far."

The maître d's lips twitched at the corners as he struggled to keep a straight face. Marcy didn't bother trying. She glanced from one man to the other and grinned.

"You've brought girls here before, haven't you?" Her voice was low and sultry with amusement.

"Women," he corrected. "Very lovely, very nice women, although never more than one at a time. Isn't that right, George?"

The maître d' gave an almost imperceptible nod. "Of course, sir. To do otherwise would be bad form." He said it in a tone that implied the present conversation was in bad form. "Miss?" He pulled out the chair opposite Jack's at the small table and gestured her toward it.

Marcy let him seat her, holding her laughter until he'd disappeared in the direction of the lobby. "Gawd, I'll never grow up," she said between giggles. "I wanted to stick two pieces of gum in my mouth, blow a big bubble, then pop it and wink at him."

He shook his head. "Can't. Your hair's not big enough. You couldn't pull off that act without bigger hair. And dumber eyes." His own eyes sparkled with devilment. "That must have been some meeting you came from."

She grinned back at him and fluffed her curls. "Like it?"

"What's not to like? I haven't seen that much leg on you since you outgrew that yellow sunsuit with ruffles across your bottom."

"You can't remember that. We couldn't have been more than two years old."

"I remember the pictures. You had great legs even back then."

"You never said so."

"I never knew you wanted me to."

She stared down at the tablecloth and picked at an almost imperceptibly small speck of lint. "I wanted you to. When I was fourteen, I had the biggest crush on you. And you had the biggest crush on Penny Bartow, who had the biggest—well, you know."

He reached across the table, lacing his fingers between hers. "You're kidding me, right?"

She shook her head, knowing he wasn't referring to Penny Bartow's obvious attributes.

"I never knew." He glanced up, noting the approach of the wine steward. He didn't release her hand, though, as he consulted her about the wine, then ordered a bottle sent to the table. "I wish I'd known."

"I'm so glad you didn't," she replied, squeezing his hand. "I'd have been mortified if you found out, because I knew I wasn't your type and you'd never want to speak to me again. And after watching you make a fool of yourself over Penny, I decided I liked you a whole lot better as a friend than as a boyfriend."

"And now?"

"And now I think I have an even bigger crush on you," she confessed.

"And?" he prompted. "Am I better as just a friend?"

She knew how she wanted to answer, but the situation wasn't so simple. It wasn't a perfect world, and theirs was a complicated relationship. "So far so good," she replied.

He nodded. "My thoughts exactly. Who's the new client?"

His abrupt change of the subject startled her for a moment, until she noticed what she suspected might be a flicker of jealousy in his expression.

"What are you talking about?"

"The woman at your office said you'd be coming straight from a meeting. That isn't your usual dress-for-success outfit, although I do recall a conversation we once had concerning tailoring your image to the expectations of the client."

"And I look like I've been checking out Hugh Heffner's mainframe?" she suggested, then relented. "There's no client. I just thought I'd have some fun and surprise you with a drop-dead new look. After all, I no longer have to consider the reputation of my dinner partner. Yours is already tarnished beyond retrieval," she told him with a naughty smile.

"As I'm sure George will testify." He picked up the menu, perused it briefly, then glanced at her over the top. "We could skip dinner and go straight to the main event. I'm sure George would understand."

She arched her brows in a frosty rejection of that idea. "Don't let the dress fool you. This is the first time you've invited me here, and you're not getting off cheap."

He sighed. "I didn't think so," he said, leaning sideways to steal a glance at her legs. She resisted the urge to tug the hemline of her dress lower. She felt self-conscious enough without drawing further attention to herself. At the same time, she couldn't suppress a thrill of excitement at the startled delight in his gaze every time he allowed it to slip to her legs.

Hadn't she read somewhere that the secret to keeping a man interested was to keep him off balance with an occasional surprise, preferably a sexy one? A flutter of unease distracted her attention from the menu. Is that what she was doing? Dressing up to keep Jack from getting bored with her too quickly? The thought disturbed her, because she was honest enough to admit, at least to herself, that there probably was a smidgen of truth there.

"How's the fish here?" she asked.

"The fish? Now there's the Marcy I know and love," he replied. "The fish is excellent, although not so excellent as a freshly caught trout grilled over a fire next to a mountain stream."

She pursed her lips, trying to concentrate on the menu as his words echoed through her mind. *The Marcy I know and love.*

*It's just a figure of speech, ninny,* she told herself.

"And the Beef Wellington?" Marcy asked aloud, keeping her tone even, as if she were concerned about nothing more than the food she was about to order.

"Better than Mom's pot roast, which actually is saying a lot." Lizzy's pot roast was famous in Bridgeton. Lonely widowers and bachelors had mown her lawn and cleaned out the gutters for two weeks running in the hope of an invitation to Sunday dinner.

"Stay away from the scallops, though," Jack advised. "Nasty sauce, full of capers and hot enough to cauterize your entire intestinal tract."

"Then I'll have the beef."

"Me, too," he replied, then began to question her about the dress. Where had she bought it? When? And exactly how long did she intend to keep it on?

"Through dinner, at least," she replied, laughing.

They laughed and teased throughout dinner, and Marcy noticed he seemed happier, more comfortable with himself. He hadn't completely lost his jaded, cynical edge, but it had definitely softened. That fact was never more apparent than when a gorgeous blond approached their table with her dinner companion. Marcy recognized the woman as one Jack had dated a couple of years ago. Polished and sophisticated, Angie was the epitome of everything Marcy was not, and she was so nice that Marcy had felt guilty for resenting her.

"Angie, it's good to see you," Jack murmured, standing to greet them. "I heard you got married. Is this the lucky man?"

"Ed Holden," the man said, offering his hand before Angie could answer. Angie smiled gratefully up at the man, and Marcy noticed a thin band of pale skin where her wedding ring should be.

"Ed?" A puzzled frown pulled at Jack's brows. "I thought—" he winced as Marcy's foot connected with his shin. Her warning stare silenced whatever he'd been about to say, and he cleared his throat, stalling for a few seconds. "Well, never mind what I thought. You know how bad my memory is. Nice to meet you, Ed. Angie, you remember Marcy, don't you?"

Angie smiled. "Of course. Jack always said you could work a trout fly better than any woman on earth. Odd the things that stick in the mind, isn't it? I used to be jealous of you, can you believe it? He spent so much time with you I found it hard to believe you were like one of the guys."

Marcy tipped her head back and aimed a sweet smile in Jack's direction. "That's me. Just your average tomboy-next-door type." To punish him, she shifted, letting her skirt hitch higher up her thighs. The subtle flare of his pupils indicated he'd noticed.

Ed had, too, judging from the gleam that entered his eyes as he smiled down at her. Angie ignored him and laid a hand on Jack's arm. "It was nice to see you again. It's been too long." She practically purred the words, and Marcy felt the rise of an unwelcome surge of jealousy.

"I believe your waiter is looking for you," Marcy said, glancing back in the direction from which they'd come. "Have you ordered yet? I hear the scallops are wonderful." The guilt she'd once felt for resenting Angie dissolved into thin air.

Jack's brows arched with amusement. "The reviews are mixed," he said. "Ed, nice meeting you. Angie, give us a call sometime and we'll make a foursome of it." He reached for Marcy's hand and kissed the back of it, making it very obvious whom he intended to be paired with should that occur.

Angie's eyes widened almost imperceptibly. Then she turned a cool smile in Marcy's direction. "Wouldn't that be nice?"

After the others had returned to their table and Jack resumed his seat, he took a long sip of wine, then leaned close. "The scallops are wonderful?"

Marcy shrugged. "She was coming on to you."

"I didn't notice. Besides, she's married, although obviously not to that guy. I wonder what the story is there."

"He's probably her lawyer."

He took a sip of his wine. "What makes you say that?"

"No ring, but she still has a ring mark. I'd have pegged him for the other man if he hadn't been staring so hard at my legs."

"They are nice legs," Jack interjected.

Marcy allowed herself to bask in the pleasure of his admiration, although only for a few seconds. "Angie has nice legs, too, as I'm sure you know. No, there's something else going on there. Kind of sad, don't you think? She can't have been married for long."

Jack didn't answer, just stared pensively into his wine. The silence stretched between them, making Marcy wish the blasted woman had stayed at her own table and left them alone.

"It wouldn't be that way for us," Jack said at last.

She didn't pretend not to know what he meant. "We don't know that."

"I do," he insisted.

* * *

They drove down to Bridgeton together the following weekend, ostensibly to celebrate Lizzy's birthday, but also to break the news to both their mothers that the two of them had been dating. Jack thought they'd probably already figured it out, but he supposed Marcy was right. They owed the two women the courtesy of an explanation. Otherwise, they'd worry and speculate themselves into early graves.

Jack was not looking forward to telling his mother, not after the lecture Lizzy had delivered when she'd heard about that kiss during the Rose Festival. She'd feel obligated to deliver all sorts of dire warnings, and he simply didn't want to hear them.

He was grown up enough, finally, to understand exactly what he needed to do. All he had to do was convince Marcy.

"Almost there," he said, nudging her awake. She'd dozed off about ten minutes out of the city, which was no surprise considering how little sleep the two of them had gotten the night before.

She yawned and stretched. "Darn it, and I was having such a good dream."

"About me?"

She smiled lazily. "What do you think?"

"And was I good?" He winked broadly, anticipating her playful slap against his arm. "I was, wasn't I?"

"You're very, very bad, and you know it," she replied, although he could tell from the faint flush in her cheeks he was right. She'd been dreaming about him, and it hadn't been a platonic situation.

"How do you think the mothers are going to take

the news?" she said. The faint thread of tension in her tone revealed her nervousness. He couldn't blame her. Half the town was probably still talking about their last visit and that scene at the church.

"I think they'll start sewing baby clothes," he said. "Would that be so bad?"

She crossed her arms and cast an irritated glance in his direction. "You're just baiting me. I know it and you know it, so you can stop it."

He pursed his lips, opting for silence. When all else failed, shut up, his grandfather used to say. Good advice, he decided.

Both women were waiting on Cecilia's front porch when Jack turned the car into his mother's driveway. Neither got up, preferring to call their offspring over instead.

"Jack, dear, there's lemonade in the refrigerator. Bring that, too, when you come," Lizzy ordered.

"I guess that means I'm supposed to get the glasses." Marcy squeezed his hand, then took a deep breath as if steadying herself for a monumental task.

"Out of the frying pan and into the fire," he replied. "Let's get this over with."

The mothers took the news better than either of them expected. In fact, their matter-of-fact response would have been a letdown if they hadn't extended their motherly advice into matters of an intensely personal nature.

"That's nice, dears," was all Cecilia had to say. "And you're using protection, I presume."

"I—I—" Marcy stuttered and looked to Jack for help. He rolled his eyes and asked Cecilia if it really was any of her business.

"Of course it is," Lizzy interjected. "We both know what it's like to raise children alone."

"It wouldn't be that way," Jack said. He ought to make a recording so he could simply tap a button and play it back whenever the circumstances called for it.

The two older women glanced at each other and nodded knowingly. "So speak the young," Lizzy said. "Honey, we all think we're different, and then we find out we fall into the same puddles as everybody else. Heck, I'm surprised this hasn't happened before now, considering all the time the two of you spend together. Two young, healthy bodies, always hanging around together. Something's bound to develop."

Marcy looked pale. He wasn't sure if she was about to faint from embarrassment or explode with outrage. He didn't want to find out, not this early in the weekend.

"I think I'll take a walk," he said, holding out his hand. "Marcy?"

"That sounds like a good idea. We can unload the car later."

"Be careful, dears," Cecilia called after them.

"Don't do anything I wouldn't do," Lizzy added.

"Don't do that, either."

He caught Marcy's grimace and groaned. "We've died and gone to hell, haven't we?"

Jack couldn't sleep. He wanted to blame the old mattress, the pillow, the lack of air-conditioning in the tiny bedroom he'd occupied from his earliest memories until he'd left for college. The truth was there simply was too much space in the narrow bed. He missed Marcy.

It wasn't the sex, although that was pretty terrific. Just the thought of Marcy naked beside him made him grow hard with desire. What he missed most, though, was the sound of her breathing, the sweet warmth of her body curled next to his, relaxed and trusting.

Weird how in a few short weeks his whole world had turned on end, simply because he'd finally opened his eyes to what had been there all along.

Too restless to lie there alone staring at the ceiling, he rolled out of bed. Slipping on a pair of jeans, he glanced out the window. Moonlight filtered through the thinned branches of the dying elm in the side yard, throwing eerie shadows across the grass. A light breeze hissed through the dimness, followed by the call of a night bird.

Moving quietly so as not to wake Lizzy, Jack padded through the house, his feet bare. He swiped a beer from the fridge, popped off the cap, and took a long drink as he headed out the back door. He slumped into a deck chair and stared up at the stars. He passed a good half hour picking out the constellations and counting falling stars. After the sixth one, he abandoned his beer and stole around the corner of the house to knock on Marcy's window.

Unlike him, she apparently had no trouble sleeping. The idea irritated him. He knocked again, but with no better results. He didn't dare pound louder for fear of waking Cecilia.

Finally, he retrieved a screwdriver from the toolbox in his car and used it to dislodged the screen from the window frame. He shoved the window open as wide as it would go and tossed a fat rose blossom at her. It landed on her nose, then slid down her cheek to the pillowcase. She jerked upright, sputtering. Then she sneezed hard.

"Shhh. Do you want to wake up the whole neighborhood?" he whispered.

"Jack?" She stared at him, her eyes still drooping with sleepiness.

"You were expecting someone else?"

She sneezed again and grabbed a tissue from the box on the bedside table. "I was having this great dream," she began, then paused to blow her nose. She took just long enough for him to imagine what sort of dream he hoped she'd been having, long enough for his jeans to tighten uncomfortably.

"I'd just hooked the granddaddy bass at that place where we went on the picnic," she continued. "Then something jumped out of the water and whacked me in the face." A delicate shudder shook her shoulders, and she grimaced, then rubbed at the bridge of her nose, remembering. "Did you drop something on me?"

"From clear over here?" The bed stood against the far wall, at least ten feet from the window.

"What was it?" She gingerly felt the pillow. Her fingers jerked back when she touched the flower, due, no doubt, to the influence of that dream. She probably half-expected to find a wet, scaly fish resting on her pillowcase.

"It's a rose—dethorned, of course. Get dressed. You're missing the meteor shower."

"Huh?" She lifted the rose to her face and inhaled

deeply. Surprised pleasure softened her expression, reminding him of the way she'd looked the first time they'd made love. He wished he could climb through the window and make love to her now. She looked so beautiful sitting there, her hair tousled, her eyes closed, her expression a vision of dreamy wonder.

Strange that in all the times he'd stood here at this window, trying to talk her into one stunt or another, he hadn't noticed how tempting she was. Correction—he'd noticed, but he'd never allowed the notion more than a passing thought. For one thing, she'd have slapped him silly if he'd tried anything. For another, he'd have lost his best fishing buddy.

No, the time hadn't been right until now. For either of them.

She fluttered her fingers around the flower, loosening several petals. As they floated to the floor, he remembered why he'd come for her.

"Falling stars," he said, his tone low and rough with emotion.

She glanced up from the flower, her delicate brows knit in puzzlement. "What did you say?"

"Falling stars."

Her expression cleared. "Much better. I thought you said 'fall on Mars.' I thought maybe I'd better pinch myself to see if I was awake or stuck in some weird dream about seasonal tours to other planets."

"Nope, you're awake. I'm standing between your mother's rosebushes, and there's a meteor shower tonight. I've seen six already."

She sat up a little straighter. "For real?"

"Remember in high school when we sat up all

night with your Dad's camera on the tripod, taking pictures for my science report?" She'd been relentless, worse than his mother when it came to nagging him to keep his grades up.

"It's been years since I sat out just to watch the stars," she said. Anticipation sparkled in her eyes. "Want me to bring a blanket to lay on? And maybe a little bug spray? No sense in letting chiggers and mosquitoes ruin the experience."

"You read my mind, sweetheart. Meet me at the back door."

He waited a minute more, watching her flip back the sheet and pad across the hardwood floor toward her suitcase. Halfway there, she glanced back and grinned. "You'd better get going before the police drive by and mistake you for a peeping Tom." Then she pulled down the windowshade in his face.

With the screen out, he could have reached back in and snapped it open with one flick of his wrist. He grinned in the darkness. It was enough to know he could do it. Let her think she'd won this round. He'd have her beside him soon enough. A blanket, moonlight, falling stars, and Marcy in his arms. Not a bad way to spend a Saturday night.

A few minutes later, the squeak of the screen door alerted him to her presence. "Jack? Where are you?" She closed the door behind her with barely a click and stepped into the moonlight. She wore running shorts and a loose tank top, and if the faint jiggling of her breasts was any indication, she hadn't bothered with a bra. Moonlight and a bra-less Marcy—life was good.

He stepped out of the deep shadow of the tool shed and smiled at her. "My yard or yours?"

"Definitely yours. Mom pruned some of the roses today, and there might be a thorny stub or two lying around in inconvenient places."

"Good point," he said, reaching for her.

She thrust a box in his hand, then shifted the rolled quilt she'd draped over one arm and handed him a chilled, sweating block of plastic-wrapped squishy stuff.

"Please don't tell me this is revenge for that flower." He lifted it to his nose, then let his shoulders relax in an exaggerated sigh of relief. "Cheese spread?" he guessed hopefully.

"Mom's garlic and jalapeño cheese log. There's a knife tucked into the cracker box."

"Mmmm. Munchies. Excellent idea." He headed for the gap in the hedge between the two yards. "You didn't tuck something to drink into the box, did you? A little mineral water to chase down the jalapeño fire?"

"Plain old tap water isn't good enough for you anymore?" She nudged him out of the way and slipped through the gap in the hedge.

"Just considering your highly sophisticated palate." He followed her through the hedge and chose a spot a good fifty feet from the deck.

"That wasn't a dig, was it?" She glanced back over her shoulder, her brows arched in a warning. "Because if that was a dig, me and my crackers and cheese logs and quilt can go back inside." The faint quiver at the corners of her mouth revealed the mirth that hovered just beneath her attempt at sternness.

"You mean you're ready to roll in the dirt with the rest of us common folk?"

She snorted, then clapped a hand over her mouth, startled by the sound.

"Apparently that's a yes. You take care of the bug spray and the blanket. I'll seek liquid refreshment."

"Oops!"

"You forgot the bug spray." He kissed her quickly, catching her by surprise. As she mouthed an involuntary "Oh," he took swift advantage, deepening the kiss. He loved the way she leaned against him, her breasts soft and unbound, her lips moving with warm abandon.

"I thought we were supposed to be watching the stars," she said after a moment. "And that you were getting us some water."

"Just kissing you good-bye."

"For a short walk to the kitchen?"

He nuzzled her neck, then planted a kiss behind her ear, delighting in her soft gasp of pleasure. "I miss you. All the time, I miss you."

"It's only to the kitchen," she said, with a breathy giggle.

"It's twenty paces. Anything could happen."

She delivered a playful shove. "Get moving. I'm thirsty. And I'm missing the light show."

"Hmmph."

With another push, she sent him on his way.

He retrieved a liter of bottled water from the refrigerator, then hesitated and swiped a bottle of Lizzy's wine as well. He paused at the back door, listening. He heard only silence. Then a gentle snore drifted through the darkness. Good, he hadn't awakened Lizzy. On the way out the door, he grabbed the radio from the counter.

Outside, he found Marcy lying on the quilt, her fingers laced behind her head as she stared up at the stars. "You missed a big one. It flashed halfway across the sky before it burned out," she told him, her eyes sparkling more brightly than the stars as her gaze shifted to his face.

"Yeah?" He knelt on the quilt beside her and handed over both bottles. "Your pick," he said. He tuned the radio to a classical station, then set it on the quilt's edge.

"Mmm, background music," she murmured. "And Lizzy's special brew." She set the wine in the grass and twisted the top from the water. She took a long drink, then screwed the top on. "Much better. Kissing makes me thirsty."

"I'll remember that."

"Do." She set the water aside and reached for the wine. "No corkscrew?"

He pulled it from his back pocket and grinned.

"I suppose you have glasses back there, too." She handed him the bottle, letting him twist out the cork.

"Don't need them. It's sexier to drink out of the bottle." He pressed his lips to the rim and tipped it up, holding her gaze as he swallowed a sip. "Almost like a kiss."

She shook her head, tutting softly. "Shame on you. Trying to seduce me in your mother's backyard."

"Am I succeeding?"

She took the bottle from him and ran her tongue lightly around the rim. Desire punched him, hard and hot. "What do you think?" she asked. She took a sip, then froze, her gaze shifting slightly. "There's another falling star. No, two! Look, you fool. We can fool around anytime. It's not every night there's a meteor shower."

She leaned backward on her elbows, cradling the bottle against her hip. He took it from her, letting his fingers brush lower and longer than necessary. "Don't think I didn't notice that," she said, amusement humming in her tone.

"You'd better have." He settled back onto the quilt and pulled her closer, fitting her against him more comfortably, or at least as comfortably as he could manage on the slightly bumpy ground of his mother's backyard. "Shut up and watch the show."

He tried to concentrate on the stars. Really. He actually managed it for a minute or two when three meteorites fell in quick succession. The rest of the time, however, he was acutely conscious of her warmth beside him, the clean fragrance of her hair, the subtle apple scent of the soap she'd showered with, every tiny movement, every subtle shift of her body.

They passed the time between meteorites with reminiscing, sipping Lizzy's wine, fabricating warped legends about the constellations, and speculating about how the blue veins got in blue cheese. A good half hour passed without a visible falling star. The concert on the radio segued into a news program.

"I guess this is intermission." He tickled the soft flesh on the inside of her arm. "What should we do?"

She poked him in the ribs. "Shut up and kiss me."

"You always were a pushy broad," he said, then kissed her before she had a chance to call him a regressive caveman jerk or something equally appropriate.

She tasted of wine, wishes, and all the promises he'd never been able to make. All the promises he wanted now, the ones he wanted to make, the ones he wanted from her.

He shifted, rolling her on top of him so his hands were free to explore. He knew every inch of her, but he needed to touch her just the same. She moaned deep in her throat, returning his passion with an equal measure.

He was barely aware of the end of the news program and the resumption of the music. The sound seeped through him, blending into the night, into the cadence of their movements. He pushed up her shirt, kissing a pathway toward her breasts. He circled one nipple with his tongue, teasing it to a peak, then turned his attention to the other.

The music blared, jolting them both. He wasn't sure whether he'd bumped the radio or she had. Jack reached for the radio at the same time Marcy did, and they bumped foreheads.

"Ouch! Sorry."

"Same here."

He started to reach again, bumped it, and knocked it over.

"Oh, for the love of—" Marcy finished with a frustrated growl, and they both fumbled for the switch.

Lizzy's back porch light switched on. Then the floodlights next door came on.

Marcy finally found the volume on the radio and turned it down. A flashlight beam arced across the grass and halted directly on them. She gasped, frozen in shocked silence, poised in a crouch as she stretched across Jack's body, her shirt still hitched high across her chest, exposing one naked breast.

# TWELVE

Marcy yanked at the corner of the quilt, covering herself. A strangled exclamation sprang from her throat.

"Mr. Radcliffe?" she heard Jack say. He sounded as surprised as she was, but there was no possible way he could be half as embarrassed. She let the radio slide to the grass and struggled to tug her shirt back in place.

The light shone full in her face, coming from the direction of the low fence bordering the back of Lizzy's yard. Then the light switched off, and a low chuckle filled the night.

An elderly man stood silhouetted in the glare of the floodlights from the house behind Lizzy's. "Goodness gracious, I thought I'd seen the last of this kind of shenanigans when you grew up and left home, Jack Rathert. That you, Marcy?"

"Just dig a hole and bury me now," she muttered.

"Oh, that's right," Mr. Radcliffe continued. "I heard something 'bout the two of you at church a few weeks ago. Didn't believe it at the time."

Jack cleared his throat. "Sorry to have disturbed you, sir. A little accident with the radio."

"Well, don't let it happen again," the older man replied mildly. "The neighborhood's full of old folks who need their sleep."

He turned and headed toward his house, whistling off-tune. Marcy's grip on the quilt eased, and she let it slide back to the ground. "Well, that was a new experience—for me, at least," she muttered. She leaned against Jack, and felt the tremble of laughter in his shaking shoulders before the sound escaped him. "And what could possibly be so funny?"

"Pull-on pants. He had them on backward."

"I didn't notice."

He shifted, pulling her into his arms as he leaned back. She rolled onto him, more from momentum than intention. "I'm sorry," he whispered. "I should have been more careful about the radio."

"Not to mention my clothes."

His hands slid to her waist, slipping beneath the fabric to spread against her back. "I'm not sorry about that, just sorry Mr. Radcliffe caught us."

Marcy drew a deep breath, preparing to admit to the same, when she heard a disgusted snort from the direction of Jack's house. "What was that?"

He groaned. "I believe my mother is awake."

Marcy rolled off him and lay on her back, her eyes shut to the twinkling show in the sky. "I think the universe is trying to tell us something."

The screen door squeaked open, then thunked closed. Lizzy's heavy steps sounded on the wooden decking, and the rail creaked beneath her weight as she leaned on it. "Jack, come inside and let the girl go home and get some rest. Maybe the rest of us can get some rest then, too."

# THE BRIDE'S BEST MAN

Marcy covered her eyes with her hands, sighed, then pushed herself upright. "Hello, Lizzy. Sorry to have awakened you."

"Not to mention half the neighborhood. Jack, I thought you outgrew this kind of behavior."

Marcy held out a hand, helping him up. "Yes, shame on you," she told him, with a wry expression. A thread of tension laced beneath the humor in her words.

He held onto her hand, pulling her along behind him as he strolled toward the porch. "Just watching the meteorite shower, Mother."

"Umm-humm." She didn't sound convinced. He didn't care. He was years past explaining his actions to his mother. His only concern was the embarrassment Marcy had suffered and the lingering tension in her stiff posture.

"I'm sorry we woke you, Lizzy."

The older woman tapped her fingernails against the deck railing, and her grim expression eased slightly. "Seems like old times, although it used to be the two of you sneaking off to steal strawberries or watermelons. Tonight, though"—she shook her head and actually made a tutting sound. "All I can say is I've never seen this side of you, Marcy."

"Not funny, Mother," Jack snapped.

Marcy squeezed his hand before he could say anything more. "Never mind," she murmured. "This is really awkward, and since I can't think of anything intelligent to say, I think I'll call it a night." Marcy unlaced her fingers from his and pulled from his embrace.

"Marcy, don't go just yet."

She backed away. "We can talk some more tomorrow. I'm tired now. I think I'll get Mom's quilt and head in."

"I'll help," he said.

She didn't wait for him, just hurried back to the quilt and rolled it quickly into a bundle. She was reaching for the radio when he caught up with her. "I'll take care of that," he said, touching her.

She nodded, then fumbled awkwardly with the quilt. "Tell me I'll laugh about this tomorrow."

He kissed the tip of her nose. "Maybe the next day."

She nodded and turned to go.

"Marcy?"

She hesitated, glancing back over her shoulder. "It was nice tonight, before the radio thing," she said.

He nodded. "It was. See you in the morning."

When he returned to the house, he found his mother had already gone inside. She hadn't gone back to bed, unfortunately. She waited in the kitchen, one foot tapping restlessly, her hands fiddling with the corner of the tablecloth.

"Marcy's not like other women," she blurted out. "You can't just have your fun and then move on when you get bored."

"That's why I don't intend to move on. Marcy's all I need," he told her.

Lizzy glared at her son. "And what are you going to do when this burns out? What am I supposed to say to Cecilia when she comes to me, all upset and worrying about her daughter?"

Unruffled, Jack smiled at his mother. "It won't burn out."

## THE BRIDE'S BEST MAN

"Hmmph." Lizzy tapped the tabletop nervously. "If it does burns out—and with your history, that's a very likely prospect—maybe we'll all be lucky and Marcy will be the one dumping you."

Jack stilled, unsettled by the thought. It wasn't as if it hadn't occurred to him. He'd been shoving it into the back of his mind, ignoring it for weeks, refusing to give credence to the possibility.

But it was possible.

Here, with his mother seated opposite him, blunt honesty in her eyes, he faced the truth. He might not convince her. Worse, she might decide that the last few weeks, however spectacular, were nothing more than a fling. Maybe he *was* her rebound relationship.

"If that happened, I really don't know what I'd do."

Lizzy's expression softened. "Son, you'd do what you've always done, what we all do. You'd just go on. Think of it this way—when the passion fades, at least the two of you will still be friends. That's a lot more than your father and I could manage." A sadness flickered in her eyes. "That's a lot more than I've had with any man."

Jack shook his head. "I don't think we could go back to what we were before. It would always be there between us. I don't think we could stay friends at all."

The casual, easy trust they'd shared wouldn't survive. He knew that as surely as he knew his own name. He also knew when Marcy gave her heart, she gave it completely and expected the same in return. He'd discovered he was the same, too. For the first time in his life, he'd given his heart to a woman he loved.

"No, Mom, it simply couldn't happen."

The creak of a board on the back deck alerted him that they weren't alone. He turned to find Marcy at the screen door, her expression stiff and unreadable. He wondered how much she'd heard.

"Sorry. I heard voices and knew you were still up." Her tone was so cool he was sure she'd heard something that had disturbed her. She held up his car keys. "They must have fallen out of your pocket. I found them rolled up in the quilt."

"Thanks, but you didn't need to bring them over," he said as he opened the screen door and took them from her extended hand. "It could have waited until morning."

"I see that now," she said, turning away. She hurried down the steps, her back stiff.

"Marcy?" He caught up with her at the corner.

She flinched as his hand touched her arm, and he thought he saw the glimmer of tears in her eyes before she turned her face away. "I'm sorry to have interrupted. I knew I wouldn't be able to sleep after—well, you know. I guess I was just looking for an excuse."

"How much did you hear?"

"Enough. We've screwed it up, haven't we?"

"No. I was just trying to explain to Mom, and she was being dense on the subject. As usual."

"You said we couldn't go back to being friends."

"Not like before," he agreed.

"So we *have* screwed it up."

He sighed. "Only if we let it be that way."

She shook her head, resignation tightening her features into an unreadable mask. "It's like you said. It won't ever be the same. We're just running on lust and borrowed time. It's fun now while it lasts, but when it's over we'll be stuck with nothing."

"It's more than that," he insisted. "It has to be."

She sighed, and within that sound was a wealth of meaning. Emotions he couldn't begin to put into words, but felt vibrating between them just the same. Her eyes, those beautiful, soft brown eyes, shimmered with unshed tears as she spoke.

"Sometimes I can convince myself of that for a couple of days at a stretch. Sometimes it all seems so right. We've always been friends, and the last few weeks"—her voice grew husky, and heat flared in the depths of her gaze. "The last few weeks have been too good to be true. Pure heaven. No matter what, I can't regret anything that's happened with you."

She leaned close, raising herself on her tiptoes to kiss him. He tasted her tears on her lips and wrapped his arms around her, holding her tightly against him. "Don't cry," he whispered.

"I'm not crying," she lied. She cupped her palms around his face, studying him in the filtered moonlight beneath the dying elm tree. "It's useless to cry about things we can't change, right? That's how life is. Life just happens, and it's up to us to go with the flow."

"I thought that's what we've been doing." He smiled tightly, trying to inject a little lightness, trying to ignore the knot growing in the pit of his stomach.

She tilted her head to the side, looking sad. "You're right about that much." She backed away, letting her hands fall to her side. "The trouble is, it's not something I'm very good at."

"Then marry me."

The wind fluttered the branches overhead, disturbing the pattern of shadows, rustling the leaves. The sound was like a sad sigh heaved from the depths of the earth.

"You know that's not the answer," Marcy said. She turned away and hurried inside her mother's house, leaving him standing alone in the darkness. Very alone.

Marcy didn't join them at church the next morning. He wasn't sure whether she'd simply been tired, as Cecilia insisted, or whether she didn't want to be in church with him. He could think of a number of reasons why—the scene they'd created the last time they'd attended, the prospect of facing Mr. Radcliffe in broad daylight, her doubts about the rightness of the two of them together.

She did join them for lunch in Cecilia's kitchen, but she seemed subdued. Shadows lingered beneath her eyes, despite her having reportedly slept in. "You all right?" he asked in a low voice as Lizzy and Cecilia exchanged the gossip they'd individually garnered after church services.

She smiled, although her expression seemed strained. "I'm fine. Just a little tired from all the excitement last night."

"I'm sorry. I should have known better," he said, referring to the incident in the backyard. When she paled, he realized she might have placed another meaning on his words.

"I meant what I said last night and all the other times I asked you to marry me," he continued.

Marcy started to speak, then clamped her mouth closed. Jack noticed the older women had grown silent and were staring at the two of them, solemn concern in both their expressions.

An overwhelming urge to explain himself came over him. He started to speak, then clamped his jaw closed as tightly as Marcy's. Damn it, he and Marcy were adults. This was their business, and interference from those two women could only make matters worse. The incident at church the Sunday after the Rose Festival was evidence of that fact. Good intentions had sunk the best of relationships.

"More potato salad, please," he said after a moment.

Cecilia passed the bowl. "Then I can assume your intentions are honorable."

The statement sounded so archaic that Marcy burst into laughter. "Thanks, Mother, for your concern, but I think you've misunderstood. I'm the one who isn't ready to jump back on the wedding bandwagon."

"It's true," Lizzy insisted. "If you ask me, the girl shows good sense."

The bowl of potato salad thumped onto the table, and Jack shoved his chair back enough to allow room for him to cross his arms over his chest. "Thank you, Mother. Your opinion is noted for the record. Cecilia, do you have anything to add?"

Marcy cleared her throat. "Leave it alone, Mother."

Cecilia's hand fluttered against her throat. Then she lifted her chin to the stubborn angle he'd seen Marcy assume so many times. "You both know that, unlike Lizzy, I had the great blessing of a very happy marriage. I couldn't wish for anything more for my daughter. And that's all I have to say on the matter." A heavy sigh eased the stiffness from her shoulders, and she turned her attention back to Lizzy. "Should we get the dessert?"

"Huh?"

"The ice cream. It's in your freezer, remember?"

Comprehension dawned in his mother's expression. "Oh, the ice cream. Yes, yes, I'd forgotten. No room in your freezer. Why don't you come with me? You can help me with the chocolate sauce."

"Good idea. Children, if you'll excuse us," Cecilia said, rising. The two women scurried out of the house like mice with a cat on their heels.

Marcy propped her elbows next to her plate and leaned her face in her hands. "This is worse than hell," she muttered, her words faintly muffled. "This is torture by bored, manipulating, interfering—"

"And well-meaning," Jack interjected.

"—troublemaking mothers who need to get lives of their own so they don't have the time or energy to bother with ours." She straightened and pushed back from the table, then stood and began to pace. "I could just strangle them. As if things weren't complicated enough." Her crossed arms and stiff shoulders mirrored his own tense posture.

"Maybe there's a twelve-step program we can send them to," he replied. "Mothers Anonymous."

"You know what they're expecting." She halted and leaned back against the refrigerator. A sunflower magnet tumbled to the floor.

Jack retrieved it and set it beside his plate. "It's pretty apparent."

"They're giving us time to talk, and they're going

to waltz back in here and wait for the happy announcement. Only there isn't going to be an announcement, and they're going to be damned disappointed—or at least my mother is. Your mother seems to be more reasonable on this subject."

Jack let the silence stretch between them, until her restless pacing resumed. "Why don't you want to marry me, Marcy? Really?"

She crisscrossed the kitchen twice, then sank into her chair. She stared at her hands for a moment, clenching and unclenching them. Then she laced her fingers through her hair, shoving it back from her face. "You want the truth? The God's honest truth?"

"Nothing more. Nothing less."

Vulnerability shone through her frustration, and there was a faint tremble to her chin. Her eyes watered with unshed tears. "Because I'm afraid it won't last. I'm afraid you'll break my heart. And when that happens, I won't even have my best friend's shoulder to cry on."

He reached across, taking both her hands in his. His gaze intent, he willed her to see the sincerity in his eyes, to hear it in his voice. "I love you. I want to marry you." When she let her gaze fall to the tabletop, his heart sank with it. "You weren't afraid to take a risk with Roger. Why is it different with me?"

"I have more to lose," she said after a moment.

He nodded, understanding in spite of his impatience, maybe because he'd known her so long and knew she didn't make decisions impulsively, not the big ones. "There's no rush. We have all the time in the world. We can go on the way we have been until you're convinced that what I say is true."

She shook her head. "I don't think so. I think maybe that's part of the problem. Too much. Too fast. Maybe if we don't slow down there'll be no turning back until we crash and burn." A thousand doubts shimmered in the troubled gaze she raised to his.

"What are you saying?"

She drew a deep breath. "We should slow down. Not spend so much time together. If it's real, it won't fade. If it fades"—her voice cracked, and she drew another deep breath. "Then we'll know."

Marcy wished a thousand times over the course of the next week she could take her words back. She missed him more than she'd ever imagined possible.

As she packed her briefcase at the end of the day, she considered the message the receptionist had put on her desk earlier in the afternoon.

*Sorry about dinner tonight. Problems with an installation. I'll call you tomorrow.*

*Love, Jack*

She'd been in a meeting with a client when he'd dropped by and told the receptionist not to disturb her. As soon as the woman explained, Marcy had promptly ordered her to disturb her the next time. The woman's knowing smile might have bothered Marcy a few weeks ago. Now all she cared was that she hadn't seen Jack for a week and the evening she'd been anticipating stretched long and lonely ahead of her. It was enough to make her wish Jack hadn't taken her seriously when she'd insisted they needed to slow down.

Unwilling to go home to an empty apartment after work yet again, Marcy nosed her car onto the freeway. She drove out of town and, for lack of anything better to do, followed the route Jack had taken toward Martha's farm where they'd picnicked and thrown crumbs to the granddaddy bass in the pond.

The first thing she noticed as the farmouse came into view around the bend was the "sold" sign. She drove past slowly, her heart heavy for no good reason except that she remembered the pleasant little fantasy Jack had spun about the two of them raising children there. That was the trouble with fantasies, she thought. They couldn't come true, but they still had the power to make her heart clench and flutter. And even when she knew there wasn't a prayer of them coming true, it still hurt to see the proof.

Three days later, when she met Jack for lunch at a fast-food joint halfway between their separate places of work, she kept silent about the farm. "I guess business is good," she said as they sat down at a tiny table next to a family with two toddlers gumming french fries.

"Pretty good," he muttered noncommittally around a bite of burger. He chewed for a moment, swallowed, then took a sip of his drink. "We got the bid on the new Wirth Laboratories building, plus a couple of smaller projects."

"I guess that's what's been taking up most of your time," she said.

He paused, his brows arched. "You're the one who said we should slow down. Did you change your mind?"

She tapped her nails on the table, then curled her fingers into a fist in her lap when she recognized the betraying movement. "I still think it's the sensible thing to do."

"But is it what you want?"

She hesitated. "I'm not sure."

He nodded slowly. "I need to make a trip out of town this weekend. I may be gone most of next week, too—some work I need to oversee myself. When I get back, maybe we can talk—see if you're sure then."

His cool tone touched a raw spot. Since she didn't trust herself to speak, she took a bite of her sandwich. She might as well have been chewing sawdust. It seemed to stick in her throat when she tried to swallow, and even a long drink of her soda didn't help much. The problem wasn't the sandwich, she knew, but her own sense of rising dread.

"I have to go to Cincinnati on Tuesday," she told him. He glanced up, a question in his eyes. "The client is Roger's company. I have to make a presentation to the board of the parent company, do some work with the programmers, that sort of thing."

He nodded. "Roger going?"

"I think he's in London again."

He seemed pleased with that, which was some consolation. They talked of inconsequential things for the rest of the brief meal, then walked to the parking lot together.

"I do miss you," she admitted as they halted beside her car.

# THE BRIDE'S BEST MAN

"You know I miss you," he said, finishing with a quick, intense kiss that made her knees wobbly. He touched her cheek. Then, after a quick glance around the parking lot, he took a step backward. "I'll see you when you get back."

He didn't, though. She returned from Cincinnati on a Friday, but he wasn't in the office. Sally Rose was evasive about his whereabouts, and when Marcy called back later, she got the office answering machine. She didn't hear from him all weekend.

On Monday, she was leafing through a stack of paperwork and trying not to wonder why he still hadn't returned any of the half dozen messages she'd left for him when the receptionist buzzed her.

"You have a visitor," the woman announced. "Shall I send him in?"

A buzzing excitement laced through her normally cool tone, and Marcy heard a hint of that knowing tone she'd used the other day in response to Marcy's orders concerning messages and visits from Jack. It was enough to make Marcy's heart heart leap in anticipation.

"Send him in, of course."

She shoved the papers to the corner of her desk and started to rise. The door swung open, revealing Roger's immaculately dressed figure.

She froze, surprise and disappointment at war within her.

"Glad you could see me on short notice," Roger said, stepping inside and closing the door behind him. "I just got back and thought I'd deliver the good news in person on the way to the downtown office."

She returned to her chair and pasted on a cool smile. "It's good to see you again. You look well."

"You look tired," he responded bluntly.

His honesty threw her off guard. "Long hours," she responded. "You know how it is."

"And Jack? Is everything all right there?"

"We're working on things," she replied, feeling the heat rise in her complexion. She'd thought it awkward facing Lizzy after the fiasco with the radio, Jack, and Mr. Radcliffe's flashlight. She couldn't imagine anything more awkward than this moment.

"Good. He's a surprisingly decent man, and he does care for you." The sincerity in his expression left Marcy speechless. "You can tell him I took his advice and moved on. I've been seeing Sonia."

"The sister-in-law or whoever she is, the woman Ingrid brought to dinner at the restaurant?"

He nodded. "We have a lot in common. Now, for the reason I came. The board has voted to go with your company with a few minor changes to the proposal you presented. You'll find all the details in here," he continued, pulling a thick envelope from his briefcase.

They spoke a few moments about the changes. Then he excused himself and left. For a few minutes, she sat in silence, turning over Roger's news in her mind. All of it—the contract, Sonia. Especially Sonia. Not even a trace of jealousy stirred at the thought. In fact, her feelings on the subject were much closer to relief. She didn't particularly like the woman, but in all honesty, she was more Roger's type. She hoped they'd be happy together, or that he'd find happiness with someone.

# THE BRIDE'S BEST MAN 241

She picked up the phone and dialed Jack's office. Sally Rose answered again. "Just the person I wanted to talk to," she said. "I'm having a barbecue at my house Wednesday, sort of a housewarming for mother. She's pretty much moved in now, and I want to make her feel at home."

"I'd be happy to come," Marcy said, remembering the woman's generosity with the picnic she'd prepared for her and Jack.

"Good. Jack said to tell you he'll be gone most of the week, but he'll try to make it to the picnic so the two of you can talk a little."

"Anything else?" Marcy asked.

"No, that's all he said."

*Of course that's all he said, you ninny,* Marcy told herself when she'd hung up. *What did you expect? Protestations of undying love delivered through his secretary?* Even if Jack were the type, Sally Rose wasn't.

Nope, she'd simply have to wait until Wednesday to see how things stood between them. She'd find out then whether he missed her as much as she missed him, whether he was as ready as she was to go back to the pattern they'd established in the few weeks they'd been lovers.

# THIRTEEN

Jack was nowhere to be found. Marcy scanned the crowd milling around in Sally Rose's backyard for the tenth time in as many minutes for a glimpse of him, then released a frustrated sigh.

"He went with my Alfred to get some more ice," Sally Rose said at her ear. "Come on, I could use an extra pair of hands at the grill."

"Am I that obvious?" Marcy asked, taking the tray of meat Jack's grandmotherly assistant thrust at her and following her across the patio.

"Only to someone who knows what's what," Sally Rose replied. "I hear you've been pretty busy yourself these days."

"Business as usual. Besides, what else do I have to do? It's not much fun going fishing by myself." Marcy set the tray on a picnic table and helped Sally Rose arrange the various cuts on the grill as they talked.

The side gate swung open a moment later, and Jack stepped through, laden with four bags of ice. Sally Rose's husband followed with three more. Both women scooted out of the path to the ice tubs.

When they'd emptied the bags and restocked the tubs with soft drinks, Marcy slipped up beside Jack and stood on tiptoe to kiss his cheek. "Hello, stranger," she whispered.

He wrapped an arm around her shoulders and hugged her. "I guess this means you missed me a little."

"Just a little," she answered, her voice husky.

He kissed the tip of her nose, then pulled away. "I need to take care of a few things. I'll catch up with you later. Stick around. We need to talk about something important."

She clutched at his hand, puzzled by his attitude. He seemed preoccupied—not distant, exactly, but not his usual self, either. "What's up?"

He squeezed her hand briefly, then released her. "I'll explain later."

He disappeared back through the side gate, leaving her with the unsettled feeling the day would not end as she'd hoped. She turned to find Sally Rose watching her with a speculative expression.

"I hear Jack asked you to marry him and you turned him down."

Marcy lifted her chin and glared at the woman. "Is there anything you don't know?"

"He hasn't told me your bra size, but I could probably venture a guess," Sally Rose teased. A low chuckle followed when she noticed Marcy's blush. "Goodness, you're the first one he's dated who still has the ability to do that."

"Do what?" Marcy pretended not to know what she meant.

"Hmmph. So tell me, why won't you marry the man?"

Marcy fumbled with the wrapper on another package of meat. "Come on, he's not exactly the hearth-and-home type. You've known him long enough to figure that out."

"Under the right circumstances, he could be. And I know that's what you want. It's written all over your face every time you look at him. Heck, I've known for years there was something going on between the two of you. I was beginning to think you were both too dense to figure it out."

"Maybe. And maybe it's all just wishful thinking."

Amusement twinkled in Sally Rose's light blue eyes, crinkling the crow's-feet fanning out from the corners. "Not on my part. I have no vested interest in the outcome of this little scenario, with the possible exception of keeping my boss in a decent mood. I do have a few personal observations to share, if you're interested."

"Go ahead," Marcy said, knowing the woman would whether she gave her permission or not.

"You see how it is with me and my Alfred," Sally Rose said, gesturing with the spatula toward her husband. He smiled in her direction, then continued his conversation.

"We're best friends," Sally continued. "We knew each other in grade school, but his family moved away. I met him again years later after my divorce from my first husband, and we found we still had quite a few things in common. We had such good times together. How we used to laugh! We still do, you know. We have the same sense of humor—like the same kind of jokes, which helps. Mostly, though, we were good friends first, and we still are."

"Like me and Jack." Marcy couldn't contain a bittersweet smile. That's how they *had* been before they'd crossed the line from friends to lovers. Were they still good friends? She wasn't sure.

Sally Rose smile widened. "But we have the other, too. I've had two types of marriages. Let me tell you, the friends and lovers combination wins hands down. You'd be an idiot to chicken out when you can have it the first time around."

Marcy's gaze narrowed suspiciously as she scanned the yard, searching for Jack. "Is that what he told you? That I chickened out?"

"He said you had doubts about his motives."

"Wouldn't you?"

The older woman shrugged. "That's not for me to decide. All I can say is what I see every day when I get to work, and that's a man who's dragging his tail around looking about as sad as a man can look. He wasn't that way a few weeks ago. Tired, maybe, but he had the silliest grin on his face most of the time."

She flipped a burger, then nudged it toward the edge of the grill. "Hand me that platter, will you, hon?"

"Sure." Marcy did as she was asked, then chewed at her lip for an instant. "I've missed him," she admitted. "I know I told him we should back off for a while, but I didn't expect him to start avoiding me."

"Avoiding you? What makes you think that?" This time, she met Marcy's gaze square on. "Did you ask him what he's been up to?"

"He said it was a project, but he wouldn't say what." When Sally Rose didn't answer, just turned her attention to the burgers, Marcy's suspicions flared. "You know something, don't you?"

"It's not another woman, if that's what you're thinking. I know that without a doubt. You can't work with a man for eight years without learning the signs. Besides, I have inside information."

"Yes?" Marcy prompted.

"I'm sworn to secrecy. I will say this, though." She jabbed the air between them with the spatula for emphasis. "There's not a finer man on this earth—with the exception of my Alfred, of course. And Jack thinks the world of you. In his mind, the sun rises and sets with you."

"You could have fooled me," Marcy snapped. "He hardly even returns my calls lately. I've seen him twice, and not for long. Even today—especially today—it seems like he's avoiding me."

A secretive glint flared in Sally Rose's expression. "Just tending to some paperwork."

"During your party? What's so important it can't wait until tomorrow?"

The lines on Sally Rose's face shifted, rearranging themselves into a sympathetic smile. "He's being a pain, isn't he? I'm not sure whether he's trying to surprise you with this, or whether he's afraid to tell you for fear you won't like the idea. It's understandable, considering you refused to marry him."

Marcy leaned back against the cedar shingle siding, crossing her arms over her chest. "It's not that I don't want to," she admitted. "I just don't think he does. He feels guilty about my breaking off with Roger, even though I think he deliberately did all he could to make that happen." She held up a hand, halting the protest brewing in the other woman's expression. "I know he cares and that his intentions were good.

I'm grateful. He kept me from making an awful mistake. I just want to make sure we don't make one just as bad or worse."

Sally Rose rolled her eyes dramatically, then took a step closer, planting both fists firmly on her ample hips. "Consider this. In all the years you've known each other, did he ever bring a date on any of those fishing trips you took?"

"No."

"You?" She jabbed absently at a burger, testing it for doneness.

"Of course not."

"Not even for one of those Saturday mornings at the lake? Why do you suppose that is?" She flipped two more burgers onto the platter and held it out to Marcy. "Put those over on the table and track down that man and ask him, why don't you?"

The thought, once planted, dug its roots deep. When Jack returned a while later, she pulled him aside and asked him outright.

"You're kidding, right?" he asked.

When he saw she wasn't, he caught her hand and pulled him around the corner of the house. "Come on, I want to show you something."

"What?"

"Get in." He stopped at the passenger door of his car and swung it open.

"Why?"

"Because it's important I show you this. We can talk on the way there." Excitement made his eyes bright. He practically vibrated with some secret. She started to argue, then changed her mind and slid into the seat.

He snapped the door closed, then circled the car. By the time he was behind the wheel, she'd buckled her seat belt and was waiting expectantly.

"Are you going to tell me where we're going?"

He started the engine. "I bought a house."

"You?"

A frown creased his forehead. "I'm getting pretty tired of your treating me like I'm some sort of jet-setting playboy."

"I'm not—"

"You don't trust me," he snapped, not letting her finish. "You don't trust me to know my own mind or my own heart. I ought to be insulted."

She sat very still for a moment. "That's not what I intended."

"And in answer to your earlier question about bringing a date along when we went fishing—I never wanted to."

She waited until he'd negotiated the freeway ramp, then spoke again. "Why?"

He glanced across at her, his expression softening. "I never wanted to. It wouldn't have been the same." His attention swiveled to the road, then back to her. "I went fishing with other guys sometimes, but I never had as much fun as when you and I went. I didn't realize why until you told me you were going to marry Roger. You're the other half of my heart."

Although he'd turned his gaze back to the highway, she heard the sincerity in his tone, just as she'd heard it all the other times he told her how much he cared. This time, though, she dared to believe it.

Warmth flooded through Marcy. He meant it. Really. The walls she'd built around her doubts tumbled down.

"I love you," she whispered.

"I know that. But do you trust me?"

"With my life."

Her words should have eased the tension in the stiff set of his shoulders. They should have brought a smile to his face. Instead, his jaw tightened. "What about your heart?"

"That, too," she admitted at last.

He turned his head slightly, as if to gauge the truth of her words from the expression on her face. "Hold on, then," he said. He wrapped one strong hand around her smaller, softer one. Then he guided the car onto an exit ramp.

Marcy recognized the road as the one to Martha's house. "I drove out here last week. I was thinking about the picnic we had and missing you. I was halfway here before I realized what I was doing," she confessed, then cleared her throat. "The house is sold."

He nodded. "I'd heard. I have permission from the owners to borrow it for a while today. I thought it might be a good place to propose."

"Again?"

"Maybe this time I'll get it right and you'll agree to marry me." He looked so serious that tears sprang to her eyes. She blinked hard, trying to will them away. This wasn't the time to cry.

"Jack, I—"

"No," he interrupted. "Wait until we get there."

She started to protest, then felt his grip tighten

ever so slightly. "OK. I've waited this long. A few more minutes won't make that much difference."

He negotiated the narrow country road with excruciating care, making Marcy wish that his old devil-may-care attitude would return for just a few minutes. Suddenly, she was impatient to reach their destination.

The excitement built within her as they rounded the bend and the farmhouse came into sight. The realtor's sign still stood out front with the "sold" tab perched boldly on top. He pulled to a stop in the driveway and turned off the car. Shifting, he rummaged in his pants pocket.

Marcy held her breath, waiting for him to pull out the customary tiny box, knowing she'd find it hard to wait for him to say the words before blurting out her assent now that she'd finally decided. Instead, he pulled out a key ring bearing three tarnished brass keys and one silver one.

He held it out to her. "Welcome home, Marcy."

She stared at the keys, then lifted her gaze to his face. "You bought this farm?" She couldn't believe she hadn't guessed sooner. She'd been so wrapped up in worry, in her own doubts, that she'd failed to see what was staring her broadly in the face. Again.

"It's an investment," he said. "I was hoping we could live here together, raise a few kids, have a good life. Of course, if it's not to your taste, we could fix the place up and sell it, use the money to buy the house of your choice. Or condo. Whatever makes you happy."

Her fingers closed around the keys. She stared

down at them, then leaned toward him and kissed him full on the lips.

"You make me happy, Jack Rathert."

"Then you'll marry me?"

"Just try to stop me."

He laughed. "That wouldn't make a lot sense, would it? And the farm?"

"Perfect," she whispered, kissing him again.

It was a long time before either of them spoke again. At last, Jack drew back a fraction of an inch. "I was thinking a garden wedding would be nice."

"Beside the rose arbor," she agreed.

"Sooner rather than later." He slid his hands lower and unsnapped her seat belt. "I hope you don't mind that I made another purchase without consulting you, but there's a brand-new bed inside. The sheets are new, too, but I've slept on them a couple of nights when I was working out here."

She grinned. "I don't mind a bit. Let's go inside."

# BOOK YOUR PLACE ON OUR WEBSITE AND MAKE THE READING CONNECTION!

We've created a customized website just for our very special readers, where you can get the inside scoop on everything that's going on with Zebra, Pinnacle and Kensington books.

When you come online, you'll have the exciting opportunity to:

- View covers of upcoming books
- Read sample chapters
- Learn about our future publishing schedule (listed by publication month *and author*)
- Find out when your favorite authors will be visiting a city near you
- Search for and order backlist books from our online catalog
- Check out author bios and background information
- Send e-mail to your favorite authors
- Meet the Kensington staff online
- Join us in weekly chats with authors, readers and other guests
- Get writing guidelines
- AND MUCH MORE!

Visit our website at
http://www.zebrabooks.com

# COMING IN AUGUST FROM ZEBRA BOUQUET ROMANCES

### #57 BACHELORS INC: MARRYING OWEN
by Colleen Faulkner

\_\_\_\_(0-8217-6667-8, **$3.99**) On the verge of beginning a new life in a new state, Abby Maconnal is finally ready to put her shattered marriage with Owen Thomas behind her. Just a quick stop at her ex's to pick up her things, and she'll be on her way—or so she thinks. A hurricane is about to strand Abby under Owen's roof . . . in Owen's arms!

### #58 THE MEN OF SUGAR MOUNTAIN: THREE WISHES
by Vivian Leiber

\_\_\_\_(0-8217-6668-6, **$3.99**) Dashing Winfield Skylar is back home and busy showing Zoe Kinnear how to take some risks. But the biggest challenge of all comes when she reveals the startling truth about the little boy with Skylar blood. Can Win finally let go of the past—and allow this woman and child to become his future?

### #59 ASK ME AGAIN by Wendy Morgan

\_\_\_\_(0-8217-6669-4, **$3.99**) Being a bridesmaid in a stuffy wedding isn't Patience Magee's idea of a good time. And now, she has to walk down the aisle with logical, unflappable Jace Hoffman as her escort. There's only one question haunting her—when did Jace turn into such a hottie, and how can she keep from falling for her total opposite?

### #60 SILVER LINING by Susan Hardy

\_\_\_\_(0-8217-6670-8, **$3.99**) Wealthy heiress Katherine Spencer doesn't remember anything—not the tornado, the blow to her head, or even her own name. All she knows is that from the moment farmer Tom Weaver took her in, she's felt strangely at home. And when Tom wraps her in his strong arms, she starts to believe that this is just where she belongs.

Call toll free **1-888-345-BOOK** to order by phone or use this coupon to order by mail.

Name _____
Address _____
City _____ State _____ Zip _____

Please send me the books I have checked above.

| | |
|---|---|
| I am enclosing | $_____ |
| Plus postage and handling* | $_____ |
| Sales tax (in NY and TN) | $_____ |
| Total amount enclosed | $_____ |

*Add $2.50 for the first book and $.50 for each additional book.
Send check or money order (no cash or CODs) to:
**Kensington Publishing Corp. Dept. C.O., 850 Third Avenue, New York, NY 10022**
Prices and numbers subject to change without notice. Valid only in the U.S.
**All books will be available 8/1/00.** All orders subject to availability.
Visit our website at **www.kensingtonbooks.com**.

# Put a Little Romance in Your Life With
# Fern Michaels

| | | |
|---|---|---|
| __Dear Emily | 0-8217-5676-1 | $6.99US/$8.50CAN |
| __Sara's Song | 0-8217-5856-X | $6.99US/$8.50CAN |
| __Wish List | 0-8217-5228-6 | $6.99US/$7.99CAN |
| __Vegas Rich | 0-8217-5594-3 | $6.99US/$8.50CAN |
| __Vegas Heat | 0-8217-5758-X | $6.99US/$8.50CAN |
| __Vegas Sunrise | 1-55817-5983-3 | $6.99US/$8.50CAN |
| __Whitefire | 0-8217-5638-9 | $6.99US/$8.50CAN |

Call toll free **1-888-345-BOOK** to order by phone or use this coupon to order by mail.
Name_____
Address_____
City _____ State _____Zip_____
Please send me the books I have checked above.
I am enclosing $_____
Plus postage and handling* $_____
Sales tax (in New York and Tennessee) $_____
Total amount enclosed $_____
*Add $2.50 for the first book and $.50 for each additional book.
Send check or money order (no cash or CODs) to:
**Kensington Publishing Corp., 850 Third Avenue, New York, NY 10022**
Prices and Numbers subject to change without notice.
All orders subject to availability.
Check out our website at **www.kensingtonbooks.com**

# Put a Little Romance in Your Life With
# Janelle Taylor

| | | |
|---|---|---|
| __Anything for Love | 0-8217-4992-7 | $5.99US/$6.99CAN |
| __Lakota Dawn | 0-8217-6421-7 | $6.99US/$8.99CAN |
| __Forever Ecstasy | 0-8217-5241-3 | $5.99US/$6.99CAN |
| __Fortune's Flames | 0-8217-5450-5 | $5.99US/$6.99CAN |
| __Destiny's Temptress | 0-8217-5448-3 | $5.99US/$6.99CAN |
| __Love Me With Fury | 0-8217-5452-1 | $5.99US/$6.99CAN |
| __First Love, Wild Love | 0-8217-5277-4 | $5.99US/$6.99CAN |
| __Kiss of the Night Wind | 0-8217-5279-0 | $5.99US/$6.99CAN |
| __Love With a Stranger | 0-8217-5416-5 | $6.99US/$8.50CAN |
| __Forbidden Ecstasy | 0-8217-5278-2 | $5.99US/$6.99CAN |
| __Defiant Ecstasy | 0-8217-5447-5 | $5.99US/$6.99CAN |
| __Follow the Wind | 0-8217-5449-1 | $5.99US/$6.99CAN |
| __Wild Winds | 0-8217-6026-2 | $6.99US/$8.50CAN |
| __Defiant Hearts | 0-8217-5563-3 | $6.50US/$8.00CAN |
| __Golden Torment | 0-8217-5451-3 | $5.99US/$6.99CAN |
| __Bittersweet Ecstasy | 0-8217-5445-9 | $5.99US/$6.99CAN |
| __Taking Chances | 0-8217-4259-0 | $4.50US/$5.50CAN |
| __By Candlelight | 0-8217-5703-2 | $6.99US/$8.50CAN |
| __Chase the Wind | 0-8217-4740-1 | $5.99US/$6.99CAN |
| __Destiny Mine | 0-8217-5185-9 | $5.99US/$6.99CAN |
| __Midnight Secrets | 0-8217-5280-4 | $5.99US/$6.99CAN |
| __Sweet Savage Heart | 0-8217-5276-6 | $5.99US/$6.99CAN |
| __Moonbeams and Magic | 0-7860-0184-4 | $5.99US/$6.99CAN |
| __Brazen Ecstasy | 0-8217-5446-7 | $5.99US/$6.99CAN |

Call toll free **1-888-345-BOOK** to order by phone, use this coupon to order by mail, or order online at **www.kensingtonbooks.com**.
Name _____
Address _____
City _____ State _____ Zip _____
Please send me the books I have checked above.
I am enclosing $_____
Plus postage and handling $_____
Sales tax (in New York and Tennessee only) $_____
Total amount enclosed $_____
*Add $2.50 for the first book and $.50 for each additional book.
Send check or money order (no cash or CODs) to:
**Kensington Publishing Corp., Dept. C.O., 850 Third Avenue, New York, NY 10022**
Prices and numbers subject to change without notice.
All orders subject to availability.
Visit our website at **www.kensingtonbooks.com**

## Put a Little Romance in Your Life With
# Jo Goodman

\_\_**Crystal Passion**  $5.50US/$7.00CAN
0-8217-6308-3

\_\_**Always in My Dreams**  $5.50US/$7.00CAN
0-8217-5619-2

\_\_**The Captain's Lady**  $5.99US/$7.50CAN
0-8217-5948-5

\_\_**My Reckless Heart**  $5.99US/$7.50CAN
0-8217-45843-8

\_\_**My Steadfast Heart**  $5.99US/$7.50CAN
0-8217-6157-9

\_\_**Only in My Arms**  $5.99US/$7.50CAN
0-8217-5346-0

\_\_**With All My Heart**  $5.99US/$7.50CAN
0-8217-6145-5

---

Call toll free **1-888-345-BOOK** to order by phone, use this coupon to order by mail, or order online at **www.kensingtonbooks.com**.

Name_____
Address_____
City _____ State _____ Zip_____
Please send me the books I have checked above.
I am enclosing                                                    $_____
Plus postage and handling*                                $_____
Sales tax (in New York and Tennessee only)     $_____
Total amount enclosed                                         $_____
*Add $2.50 for the first book and $.50 for each additional book.
Send check or money order (no cash or CODs) to:
**Kensington Publishing Corp., Dept. C.O., 850 Third Avenue, New York, NY 10022**
Prices and numbers subject to change without notice.
All orders subject to availability.
Visit our website at **www.kensingtonbooks.com**.